B.E.S.T. WORLD
UNDER PRESSURE

SEQUEL TO ACE TAKES FLIGHT

CORY MCCARTHY

Clarion Books
An Imprint of HarperCollins Publishers

Clarion Books is an imprint of HarperCollins Publishers.
Under Pressure
Copyright © 2022 by HarperCollins Publishers
All rights reserved. Printed in the United States of America. No part of this book may be used or reproduced in any manner whatsoever without written permission except in the case of brief quotations embodied in critical articles and reviews. For information address HarperCollins Children's Books, a division of HarperCollins Publishers, 195 Broadway, New York, NY 10007.
www.harpercollinschildrens.com

ISBN 978-0-35-836214-2

Typography by Stephanie Hays
22 23 24 25 26   PC/LSCC   10 9 8 7 6 5 4 3 2 1

First Edition

For Chris,
my B.E.S.T. boxmate

LEVEL ONE:

MIDNIGHT ZONE

GRAYSON

PROLOGUE

Grayson Bix woke up from his aug surgery on the other side of the world.

He got up sluggishly and looked out the window and into a black night complete with unfamiliar stars. The crisp peaks of snowy mountains crowded the horizon like maybe he was somewhere in the Swiss Alps. He blinked, refocused. The image was fake. A three-dimensional screen. The window wasn't even a window.

How could he know that? He glanced down at his hospital scrubs and the brand-new red circle tattoo on his wrist. He was Bod augged now with VisionX, what Ace would call *super eyes*.

Speaking of, where were his friends? And why had he been taken away after his surgery? Did they know where he was? Were they worried? Had something gone wrong?

Gray used the full power of his augged eyes for the first

time, peering through the projection window to the wall and then through the forty feet of concrete beyond that. Even after managing to see through all those impenetrable things, he had a hard time believing what he found on the other side. There must be some mistake.

How could he be in the darkest zone at the bottom of the ocean?

LEO

1

HAIL MARY:
Welp . . . this better work

Leo dreamed of BESTBall.

Lime-green faces shone through a sudden blackout. Roaring cheers and their coach's shout ground over the court noise. Eyes closed tightly, Leo imagined the hardwood floor beneath their wheels, a sharp, last-minute impulse to pivot, to see through the other player's fake out and spin an interception. They could *feel* the weight of the stolen ball tucked between their knees, their gloved hands bursting with speed, driving downcourt with the arena shouting *Go go go* . . .

The daydream was so convincing that Leo jolted when a rolling wave tossed the hoverpod. Their stomach lost gravity for seconds, which was a lot less fun than it sounded but did make them forget their hunger for a few minutes.

Leo had to glare out the window to remember that

they weren't on the court or at ToP, the Tower of Power, with Gray or even home with their family.

They were bobbing on the surface of the ever-changing ocean in Grayson's stolen hoverpod, now with a dead battery. They'd been following a signal they believed was coming from Grayson on Jayla's aug, getting closer and closer . . . and then the signal had just disappeared.

Someone or something was messing with them.

Leo swallowed back center-court nerves just as a piping shout and small splash confirmed that Ace had fallen in the water. Again.

Jayla sat up from the back seat, rubbing her eyes. She'd been trying to get a signal out all night, to call friends for help. As soon as she was fully awake, she ran through the interface on her arm, the small screen that helped control her body's network.

Leo didn't have to ask to know that she was hoping for a response. Jayla's continued silence wasn't great news.

Leo cracked open the hoverpod door and leaned out to see what was happening below. The heat off the water was strong from the hazy morning sun. It stuffed up the cockpit like a blanket of humidity.

Ace was swimming like a tiny frog. He pulled himself up onto the landing gear, his clothes all suctioned to him. His light brown hair was plastered over his eyes, and he swiped at it. "I saw the shadow of a big fish! Maybe a whale!"

he said as if that explained his shout, splash, and swim.

"So you tried to catch it with your hands?" Jayla teased, leaning out the other door.

Ace looked around until he found a white line of shoestring floating near the landing gear. He scooped at the iridescent blue water until the string started to move toward him, and he nabbed it. He held it up, complete with a fishhook he'd made from . . . was that one of Jayla's barrettes?

"You're fishing." Leo was almost impressed.

"It's not the worst idea!" Ace was the only one who still believed they were doing the right thing. Leo was a little too realistic, and Jayla was *way* too realistic. The truth was that Grayson had gone missing, and they'd gone running after a faint signal that could be him, spanning the entire country, and then? They were way out at sea, with only a couple of cartons of water that disappeared faster than the contents of the hoverpod's fuel cell. And now they were going to starve in the middle of the ocean.

Or worse: be forced to eat whatever Ace caught with his shoelace.

Leo leaned back in and glanced at Jayla. They were both still impressed that Ace had been able to land the hoverpod at all, and now they were going to have to let him keep this daydream of becoming a self-taught fisherman.

"I now know why people get the MegaMetabolism

aug!" Ace's voice came up from beneath them, as enthusiastic as ever. "Imagine if we could dial our metabolism down right now."

"Need water," Jayla grumbled. She was using all her energy to keep her network running, but her aug only worked as well as her body, and they were all hungry and *really* thirsty at this point.

They'd been adrift for a whole day now.

Leo had to admit that they probably *would* munch something Ace caught at this point. They formed a question in their mind, and then combed through it a few times before asking, a nervous habit that kept them a fraction as talkative as everyone else.

"Our options?"

Jayla sighed. "Well, I was blasting an SOS to all my contacts, but the signal isn't strong, and it's hard to keep up when I'm tired. I'm afraid Bixonics will pick it up instead."

Jayla didn't have to explain. If Bixonics found them, they'd all be in *the biggest trouble.* Jayla would get her aug recalled because she'd deleted ToP's firewall when they'd left campus in order to follow Gray's signal. She wasn't supposed to even know how to do that. Not to mention that Ace's and Leo's dreams of getting augged would vanish if they were branded troublemaking runaways.

There had to be help somewhere that didn't mean getting busted.

Leo hated having so little information. "Can you send a different kind of message? A direct one that can go farther?"

Jayla chewed on her bottom lip, tan without her usual berry-colored gloss. "In theory, I could. Although I'm too thirsty. And who would we even call?"

"What about your family?" Leo asked, knowing this was no small question, no matter how quietly they asked it.

"I thought the Resistance might've been involved with Gray's disappearance, but why would they be out in the middle of the ocean?" Jayla always said resistance with a capital R. The movement was more real to her than to the others. In Leo's mind, the Resistance was little more than the people with the protest signs outside of ToP. Just upset about change and standing in the way. Emma acted like the Resistance was a secret agency, a threat to the tide of Bixonics progress, but that always seemed like melodrama for her show.

"So your parents are in the Resistance?" they asked for the first time.

"They *are* the Resistance. It's how they met and it's pretty much their entire lives." Jayla sighed even harder, so frustrated. "Even if I could get ahold of them, this is not how I wanted to go back. I always thought there'd be fireworks and a soundtrack with timpani."

Leo smiled. They liked picturing Jayla like that. All heroic and powerful. Leo didn't know the details of what had made Jayla run away to ToP. To be honest, they had a lot of trouble pinpointing why families did any of the things that families do. Their own parents were too focused on what other people thought of their lives, and their twin, Emma, was like a different species of tween.

Leo missed Gray; he always understood how hard family could be.

How hard *people* could be.

"What about direct messaging Ace's moms?" Leo suggested. Only Ace seemed lucky enough to be friends with his parents, although maybe that would change when he got older. Maybe it already had when he busted up Finn's face before they flew off. Leo still couldn't believe he'd done it.

Jayla leaned forward with a lowered voice. "I don't think it's a good idea to reach out. Not with Finn spying all the time. He's got too many connections to the Bix marketing corps. He's their favorite poster boy now. Gray didn't trust him, and that's good enough for me."

Ouch. Just hearing Leo's best friend's name stabbed at their soft feelings. Where was he? What had happened to him? Had he been saved by his mom? Stolen by a rival company? Bixonics was the biggest corporation on the planet, but that didn't mean some other business hadn't abducted the heir to the Bixonium throne in hopes of getting their hands on the secret alchemical formula.

Anyone could have taken Gray. Anyone.

"Hey, you okay?" Jayla leaned closer. "You're hyperventilating."

Leo stopped fast. They hadn't done that in years. They tucked each breath away, determined not to let their anxiety spill into this ridiculous *lost at sea* situation. "I think . . . we're close to desperate, Jayla."

Jayla was quiet for a long minute. "We're going to find Gray. If he's not okay, we're going to save him. And if he is okay, we're going to completely level him for not saying goodbye." Leo heard the words Jayla didn't say. That Grayson *would never* leave without saying goodbye. "We're going to find him," she said again.

Leo latched onto that idea as if it were a ball and their life depended on scoring.

The pilot's door popped open, and as if determined to be comic relief on some spiritual level, a very wet Ace crawled up into his seat, awkwardly clutching something in his balled-up jacket.

"You two are going to love me."

"We already do, Ace." Jayla leaned forward. "What'd you source from the water?"

He spread out his drenched jacket, revealing a matted hunk of seaweed.

"Yeah," Jayla confirmed. "I'm not eating that."

"But you eat it all the time when we have sushi!"

"When it's cleaned *and* prepared. And we don't have water, and you're *not* supposed to eat salty things when you're dehydrated. Have you two read a single book about pirates? *Treasure Island*? *Pirates of the Caribbean*?"

Leo and Ace shook their heads. The answer was definitely *no*. Superheroes, yeah. BESTBall almanacs, of course. Pirates? Like with parrots and scurvy and planks? Not in either of their canons.

Ace squirmed, a sign that he was trying not to shout. "But . . . Look!" He clawed at the hunk, breaking away the seaweed a bit at a time. The whole mass was tangled around a furry rock.

Not a rock.

"You found a coconut." Leo's mouth hung open with legit surprise.

Ace held up the treasure for all to admire. "Now we just have to figure out how to get it open. You know what's inside, Jayla?"

"I know what's inside, Ace."

Ace shook it, filling the hoverpod with a beautiful sloshing sound. "Water!"

And thus began the most complicated two hours of their lives. How could they all be smart and strong enough to get into the aug program only to fail at breaking a coconut open? Every single idea to crack the seed also seemed to mean that they'd most likely dump the water out in the process.

"What if we whacked it open in a bucket?"

"Do you have a bucket, Ace?" Jayla's tone reminded Leo

of the classical music she was always listening to, that lull in the orchestra that indicated it was about to crescendo. Of course, Ace did not have a bucket, and was asked—once again—to keep his ideas based on available materials.

Finally, Ace found a small bundle of tools in an access panel no one had discovered previously, and Leo was nominated, as the strongest of the three, to drill a hole through the husk with a screwdriver. It took another hour.

When the screwdriver finally popped through, all three of the boxmates held their breath.

Jayla looked at it with eyes wide with longing. "We should all have some."

Leo and Ace exchanged glances and shook their heads together. Leo handed the coconut back to Jayla with enormous care. Time for a Hail Mary. A last attempt on the BESTBall court to turn it all around. "Take it all. We trust you."

"Okay, I'm going to send someone a direct message. He might not be nearby, but I think he's our best bet." She took a sip from the coconut and made a face. "Ack! That is not like the coconut water from the cafeteria!" She drank the rest of it, making the same face the whole time. When she finished, Jayla handed the coconut back to Ace, then she began plugging away at her interface. Her breath was gusty and impatient.

Leo thought they might know who she was calling but didn't want to say.

Ace cradled his coconut. "Wish I could fly us away. I could save everyone if I had my wings already."

"How could you have your SuperSoar wings already? You haven't even started your second semester," Leo tried. "Besides, no one has ever figured out how to use that aug in real life. Grayson thinks no one ever will."

Ace was still staring at his coconut. Leo wondered how much of his brainpower went toward trying to figure out that one glorified aug.

Leo touched his shoulder. "Hey, now we get to whack it open." They spoke quietly, not wanting to disturb Jayla's concentration. "So we can eat the stuff inside."

"Really?" Ace whispered. "How?"

Leo smirked, knowing *exactly* how to open the coconut: treat it like a court celebration in BESTBall. Slam it against something hard. Which was *exactly* their forte.

The two of them shimmied down to the landing gear of the hoverpod. Leo dropped their knees in the water. It was so warm. By the time the sky was giving them just the best orange and purple sunset Leo had ever seen, they'd cracked the coconut open on the hard metal corner of the landing gear and were digging out pieces to nom with the screwdriver.

See? Easy as scoring.

Leo wished everything else were that easy. The setting sun painted the horizon with orange fury. A few stars blinked out from the deepening blue above. They found the brightest star in the sky and made a wish like in a story.

Wherever you are, be safe, Gray.

"Do you think Jayla's message will work?" Ace asked, crunching coconut. "Who do you think she sent it to?"

"I think—" Leo's words vanished faster than Grayson's signal had on Jayla's interface.

The star that Leo had wished on grew brighter and larger. It turned into an unmarked silver helo and dropped silently, setting down next to where the hoverpod bounced lightly on the open sea.

2

RINGER:
An advantage in disguise

The rescue happened fast. The door to the silver helo was hauled open, and an adult in a jumpsuit reached across the distance between the two vehicles, locking them together with a wire tether.

"Jayla!" Leo heard a high, firm voice call out.

"Mom?!"

Leo glanced at where Ace clung to the bobbing landing gear and they both mouthed *Mom*?

"We better get up there." Leo began to pull themself up, but they couldn't get in through the pilot's door because the silver helo was blocking it. Leo motioned for Ace to go around to the passenger side. They both scurried up together, piling in in time to find Jayla arguing with her mom.

"If you give me *two minutes* to explain I'll—"

"We don't have two minutes! Get in the helo. *Now.*"

"That was a fast rescue!" Ace had this way of talking to adults so easily. "We thought we'd have hours to kill."

"You two are staying here. Jayla is coming with us."

"I'm not leaving my friends!" Jayla shouted, but she was close to fainting, and everyone knew it.

"Their ride is inbound. We need to move quickly. You need medical attention." Jayla's mom looked a lot like her daughter, except she wore her hair in braids and her jaw was set in a way that relayed a professional and no-nonsense nature.

"Hey, how'd you get here so fast?" Ace asked. "Are you all nearby?" This was apparently the *wrong* question because all the adults started to move even faster. They hollered things back and forth, and Leo lost the thread on what was happening.

Inside the silver helo, several people sat strapped in seats along the cargo portion of the back. A couple of them were wearing Bixonics's tech jumpsuits: older, out-of-style ones from the look of them. Leo was surprised to recognize a person. A grad aug who'd been a sort of big-shot cadet two semesters ago—a fellow XConnect like Jayla.

By the time Leo had placed him, Jayla was in the helo and an adult had tossed a crate of water and snacks into the hoverpod and unhooked the wire tether. Leo blinked and the silver helo was gone. So was Jayla.

Ace broke into the food without hesitation. "What did they mean by our *ride is inbound*? Do you think . . . You don't think they'd call ToP to come get us?"

Leo didn't know how to answer that. Gray was missing. Jayla had been swept away by what Leo could only assume were Resistance people. "Ace, did you see that grad aug in the helo?"

"Oh, Amir? He's an aug wizard. He can use his XConnect without the interface. Not even Jayla can do that."

"*Yet*," Leo shoved in on their boxmate's behalf. "What was he doing in there?"

Ace paused mid-chew. "I dunno. The Resistance sort of rescues cadets, right? When they want out but don't know how to get free?"

"But he wasn't a cadet. He's fully augged. A graduate who—"

"Boat!" Ace hollered. "Look, Leo! A speedboat is approaching! You think this is our ride?"

Leo knew it was, but that didn't mean they weren't wary of it. "Ace, you need to lie. I don't know why they split us up, but it probably has something to do with Jayla. And Grayson. We have to hide what we've been up to, in case they work for Bixonics." Or in case the Resistance was as trustworthy as they appeared to be—which was not much at all. "We act like we were being young and stupid. Adults always buy that. We took the hoverpod for a joyride . . . and got lost. Then we ran out of battery."

"I'm so bad at lying," Ace squeaked. "I don't even know what I'm saying half the time."

"I'll do the talking."

"You will? But Gray said you never . . ." Ace stopped himself. And Leo stopped themself from asking what Gray had said. The speedboat was closer now, flashing the trademark Bixonics green along its shiny hull.

"We were just being dumb kids," Leo whispered, firming up the story. "We didn't know any better."

What a lie. Leo knew more than most of the adults around them. Not because adults didn't know anything, but because adults tended to forget things they didn't think they needed to *keep* knowing. Adults trimmed and pruned their understanding of the world, down and down, until it better fit the needs of their life.

By the time the boat had reached them and circled to a stop, Leo had changed their mind twice about the craft. It wasn't a speedboat. It looked like a flat-bottomed fanboat, but it was more high tech. Some kind of engine turned manually by the augged-up young adult rowing. Each time their arms spun, the whirring blades at the back spun ferociously.

"Holy augmentation," Ace breathed.

"Ahoy!" a second young adult aboard called out, one leg hitched up on the low railing. They had a Brain blue tattoo on their wrist, and they seemed to have put it on display on purpose. "We heard your distress signal. We're from an island south of here. We'll tow you back and charge up your pod."

Leo looked at Ace. This felt too lucky, but they didn't know exactly how or why yet.

Ace nearly tipped out of the open door to yell "Your boat is amazing!"

"Well, come on board then!" The rower hollered with a belly laugh.

Leo shot out a hand to grab Ace by the shoulder. "Wait, we don't know what side they're on."

"Side?" Ace looked genuinely confused.

Leo had never truly looked at it this way before, but there *were* sides. You were either pro-Bixonics and all that the corporation stood for, *or* you were swallowed up by the Resistance . . . at least, if Emma's news stories were to be believed. That's why Gray's life was so impossible. He knew what would happen if he didn't follow his dad's plan; he'd be made to disappear like his mother.

Was that what had happened to Gray?

The rower's kind voice broke through Leo's weary, tumbling thoughts. "Hey, they *are* runaway cadets! You win, Rosa."

"Stern. You've got to stop betting against a Brain. I keep saying it, and you keep forgetting." Rosa had white skin and brown hair that fell in their eyes, further disguising whichever Brain aug they must possess.

Leo checked the rower with light brown skin, Stern. Sure enough, they had a red Bod tattoo on their wrist. "Hercules," Ace hissed and ducked out the door. He crossed from the landing gear to the flat-bottomed boat before Leo could process it. Leo stayed where they were, slightly annoyed when the young adult with the Brain aug hopped out of the boat and onto the landing gear, and then took Ace's spot in the pod.

Within a minute, the one called Stern had hooked the hoverpod up to a towline and started rowing again. Grayson's hoverpod skied along behind the boat while Ace cheered like it was the best experience of his life.

The second young adult stared at them. "Hey, I'm Rosa. They/she. You are?"

"Leo. They/them."

Rosa held out their hand to shake, and when Leo took it, they pulled out Leo's wrist and checked their aug track bracelets. "Look what we got here, a superstar tri-tracker. No wonder we found you far away from where you're supposed to be."

Leo withdrew and frowned at this oddly assured person with their eyes veiled by their hair. "What's your aug?"

"It's a secret. You can't have it. Don't even try."

Leo didn't enjoy the way Rosa's brain skipped. Or maybe they envied it a little too much. "Okay, where are you taking us?" They let that one question ask a hundred other questions. Were they safe? Where were they going? Where was Jayla? Were these former cadets Resistance . . . or Bixonics? Or neither?

"I'm not with Bixonics. Neither Stern or me . . . we

don't play their games anymore." She plucked a snack out of the crate from the Resistance helo and broke into a lava bar. Leo was confused. How did she know how to answer the questions beneath their question? "Because I read people. That's my aug."

"That's not an aug choice." Leo ticked back through their mind, but they weren't Ace and hadn't memorized all the augs in every track. Which aug helped you read people? Was this iNsight? No, that was the Boost aug Ace was always messing around with and grumbling about.

Speaking of Ace, he was crowing extra loudly from the prow of Stern's weird boat. Leo looked through the windshield at several dolphins, cresting and swimming alongside Ace on the bowsprit, the most adorable, nerdiest figurehead of all time.

Leo laughed and so did Rosa. That helped things.

An island appeared, small and inconsequential in the distance, apart from a silvery steeple of light in the center, hidden beneath a drab canopy. A deepscraper. "Yes, we live there. Yes, we're really going to send you on your way as soon as your hoverpod is all set. We won't even rat you out to ToP. You can go back no questions asked."

"Do you work for the Resis—"

"And we *definitely* won't be answering that. Savvy?"

Stern quit rowing and the speed dwindled as they glided onto a white, sandy shore. Even the hoverpod coasted all the way in as if directed via magnetic control.

Leo got their knees wet when they hopped out, but they were too curious.

This was the very top of a deepscraper, camouflaged by a fake sandy shore. There was even a small hut covered in coconut husks and a few palms trees, but mostly the island held a mammoth pointed steel steeple that marked the top of something magnificent. A structure so solid that it seemed to run straight down through the ocean and into the bedrock of the sea—because it did exactly that.

Ace stood next to them, mouth hanging open. "Where are we?"

"Welcome to Atlantis!" Stern waved their large arms.

"Stern!" Rosa shouted. "I can't even with you. They're obviously not supposed to know where they are."

Stern smacked their forehead. "Right, well, you're *not* in Atlantis. Because that place is a myth, right? Totally doesn't exist."

"New Atlantis, the underwater skyscraper? The first ever *deepscraper*?" Ace gave a little hop of excitement. "But it was lost to the sea twenty years ago!"

Lost . . . or stolen?

Leo knew the second was far more likely. And more dangerous. A secret base indeed. This did not bode well, even if these two seemed cool and relaxed. What was the Resistance up to?

Stern looked to Rosa apologetically. "I didn't give it all away."

"*Yet*." Rosa sighed, rubbing a heavy metal bracelet on their wrist that looked like a mighty piece of tech and bore the Bixonics logo. For every assurance that these two were safe, there was a hint that they had a secret allegiance of some kind. These two ringers were guarding something.

"Can we go down inside the deepscraper?" Ace asked.

"No!" Stern was too quick. "Well, there's nothing safe down there. Nothing below the surface. Leaks and stuff from . . . a hurricane. Or was it a tsunami, Rosa?"

"Tsunami." Rosa checked Leo with those mostly covered dark eyes, gauging Leo's reaction. For information, right? She could just do that with her aug?

What aug was it?!

"You can't have it!" Rosa hollered at the sky abruptly and stomped off toward the small shack. "Come on! We've got astronaut chips!"

Stern got out Leo's chair, and Leo found it wasn't hard to wheel on the sand. It was a very thin layer, only meant to camouflage the steel platform around the steeple. On the far side, Leo could just make out a rocky outcropping that might have been a hangar disguised beneath a tarp. This was like a whole parking lot of secrecy.

Leo looked at the steeple again, at the way a canopy shielded it from anyone traveling through the sky. More camouflage. Why hide something dead? Something ruined?

You wouldn't.

Leo whistled for Ace, wanting to tell him their thoughts on all this, but he was having too much fun trying to figure out how Stern's boat worked.

The two of them were already pals, plugging in Grayson's hoverpod together. It would be charged within a few hours, which left Leo with the sensation of a ticking clock. A few hours to figure out how to break into Atlantis and find Jayla—because Leo was sure that this had to be the secret home base of the Resistance.

They might even know how to find Grayson.

END AROUND:
Get sneaky and proactive

Leo wheeled closely behind Rosa. They were intrigued by her. Perhaps it was the comfort of having another non-binary person around, or maybe it was the allure of the blue tattoo on her wrist. These two guards looked so young, they could have been cadets a few years ago; they might have had some of the same coaches in the program.

Leo might be able to sweet-talk them into letting them go check on Jayla . . . if Leo knew how to sweet talk.

Rosa walked fast but not as fast as Leo's wheels moved. They pushed the words out before they were ready, embracing this moment of just the two of them within earshot. "I know what this place is. I need to go below to check on my boxmate. You understand. You've had boxmates. They're family."

"Believe me, your boxmate is safer now than she's been since she started at ToP."

Leo didn't ask, but their thoughts began to chew on this new information like dry bread. Something about this place was getting tougher and tougher to swallow.

Rosa reached for the heavy door and cracked it open. She wasn't strong enough to pry it open all the way, grunting and pushing as she tried. "Stupid storm door," she muttered. "Stern! Get your Hercules butt over here."

Stern jogged up with Ace like a delighted puppy on their heels. They pulled the ten-inch-thick door open with one little finger, grinning at Ace the whole time. Leo and Rosa rolled their eyes together.

The tiny place was like a box at ToP—but for grownups. There was a stack of bunks four beds high, with a gravity lift that Ace immediately tried out over and over again. There was also a huge fridge beside a compact kitchen, and a security console that was dusty apart from two well-used buttons. Even the labels had been rubbed off. Leo leaned out over their chair arm to try to read the buttons; Rosa watched them. She seemed particularly aware of the way Leo was mapping things.

"You don't have any windows," they pointed out.

"The storms are wicked out here." Stern had the fridge open, tossing out snack bars and crystal fruit pops to the boxmates. "The sun too."

"Wicked dangerous." Rosa opened a panel on the wall that turned out to be a cabinet full of first aid supplies and tossed a bottle of RadiationRelief to Ace. "Don't forget the tops of your ears and back of your neck. You're pretty red, kid."

"It's Ace. He/him. I was fishing with my shoestring. Saved my boxmates with my catch."

"Oh yeah, we know who you are. Wait, you caught a fish in the open ocean with a shoestring?" Rosa was stumped for the first time since they'd met the two of them. Leo loved it.

"Well, no. But I found a hunk of seaweed that was hiding a coconut."

"That's one in a million!" Stern sat in a wheeled desk chair that crunched under their impressive muscle. "And what's your name?" They put a hand on their huge chest. "I'm Stern. He/him."

This was an easy question with an easy answer. And yet, direct questions always pumped up Leo's blood pressure, heating up their face. Why was this so hard? Why wasn't Gray here to speak up for the both of them? They'd managed to fire off their name to Rosa. Couldn't they just say it for this other dude?

"They're Leo," Ace said after the weird pause. Leo was almost thankful, and then he kept going, Ace-style. "They're cleared for all three aug tracks, but they haven't narrowed it down, even though they're starting their third semester after the holiday break." Now Leo really was red. Ugh, Ace. *And* he kept going. "They have no idea which aug to pick, which is probably overwhelming. Coach

Vaughn says he rarely gives a cadet that kind of free range. I've known I was made for SuperSoar since I was five."

Ace proudly showed off his red bracelet, conveniently ignoring the second one, the green one he was significantly less excited about.

"Bod forever." Ace and Stern gave each other high fives. "Coach Vaughn is still there?" Stern was delighted. "I loved that man like a dad. Even when he left me hanging in a cargo net for two hours."

"It's not as much fun to be triple tracked as you'd think," Rosa asserted, staring straight up into the air. Stern patted their back, a comforting move that only continued to remind Leo of Gray's absence.

"What do you mean?" Ace asked, glancing at Leo.

Rosa didn't answer, but Stern did. "Rosa was triple tracked too."

"Could I ask what your aug is?" Ace asked politely. Leo was surprised that they were both stumped and assumed that Rosa was about to yell bizarre sentences into the air like they had when Leo had asked.

Instead, Rosa said, "No."

"Come on, Ace." Leo wheeled toward the only door in the small place. It was cracked open and smelled grossly familiar: a locker room. "I'll help with your lotion."

Once inside, Leo shut the door by backing their chair up against it. They pointed to the mirror while Ace rubbed the ointment all over his sunburn. He should be okay now, but Leo wasn't proud of what their rescue mission had risked. The sunburn was evidence of their recklessness.

"Ace." Leo wheeled around, checking corners. "I think Jayla is below us."

"In the ocean?!"

"In the deepscraper. I don't think it's abandoned at all. I think it's in hiding. Before we head back, we have to get down there. Make sure she's okay."

Ace blinked at them. "I can't believe I'm going to say this but . . . maybe we should just do as we're told. I want to go back to ToP. If we keep busting up the rules, they'll kick me out. I need my wings! Once I have them, I'll be able to look for Gray everywhere, all the time!"

Leo gritted their teeth. "Ace. These people are being weird. And they're lying."

"How do you know?"

So many signs. Leo had been keeping a whole list in their head. Leo was always keeping lists. "Rosa already confirmed it with me. Jayla is right below us."

Ace gave a sudden, small hop. "You think we could see her! I don't like not getting to say goodbye."

"*Shhh*!" Leo should not have told him. Geez. "Time for our end around."

"Like in BESTBall when you sneaky score?"

"Yeah. We've got to find a way into the sublevels. This could be our last chance . . . before we go back to ToP." Leo knew this last part was important for keeping Ace on board.

"But what if Jayla doesn't need our help anymore?"

Leo was surprised. Too surprised for words. "What?"

"She hacked the Bixonics firewall, broke the trial aug software. She can't go back to ToP now anyway, and she's with her family, who are bound to do the best things for her, right?"

Poor Ace. So loved by his parents that he didn't know that sometimes families *don't* have your best interests in mind. Sometimes they have *their* best interests in mind. Leo learned that lesson when they were only nine. Their parents had spent an obscene amount of money to hire Dr. Bix to design prosthetics that they *did not want*. Grayson had been there that day, the only person to try to understand their discomfort, even though Leo couldn't put words to it. Grayson had spoken up for them and become their best friend and hero, all in a few sentences.

"Jayla ran away from her family for a really good reason." Leo spoke quietly. "And none of us truly know what that reason was. We can't just leave her behind without making sure she's okay."

Ace's red face was now all streaked with white lotion. He swiped and swiped at it, rubbing it in but truly making a mess. "Yeah. You're right. Sorry. And we still don't know where Gray went."

"Or if he went willingly." Leo thumped a hard fist on

the armrest of their chair. "I have a plan to get by the guards. First, we get them on our side. Talk ToP. You're good at that. Get them to relax. Second, we unplug the hoverpod. They can't send us back if the battery isn't full, right? Third, we get below and find Jayla."

Ace nodded. Leo somehow already knew that this plan was not going to work, but they couldn't stop themself from trying. Maybe it was because they couldn't foresee *how* it would fail.

If they could do that, they'd be unstoppable.

When they wheeled back out, Rosa was on the lowest bunk with their legs kicked up. They had something clutched in their hands, and Leo nearly groaned with joy. A BESTBall. Before Leo could beg to hold it—just to recenter themselves—Rosa chucked it at them as hard as anything.

Leo snagged it out of the air with one practiced arm.

Stern howled with glee. "You are *that* Leo!" He pointed to a digital frame behind him, which showed off a twinkling Tokyo skyline at night. He tapped it until it flicked to an action shot of Leo's current BESTBall team. Leo was dead center with the ball tucked between their knees, body leaning hard to make a sharp turn. "We've watched all your games. You're a legend!"

Leo turned the ball over in their hands while Ace bragged about specific scores and the championships that had all merged into one in Leo's head. Like always, they only itched to play. Winning was a perk. They were stunned to find that they actually missed ToP too and wanted to go back to their box. Would it still feel like home if Gray wasn't there?

"BESTBall captain in only their second semester at ToP!" Ace was saying.

"Want to play?" Leo glanced at the two guards with a hard dare in their eye.

"Do we!" Stern shouted.

And that was how they spent their day on the surface of Atlantis, shooting the BESTBall back and forth. Stern chucked it so hard that Leo needed to fake only one missed catch for the ball to go careening out into the ocean. Stern went for a swim to retrieve it, and when Ace asked for his thirtieth curly crunch bar from Rosa, Leo rolled to the hoverpod and discreetly unplugged it.

Ace had truly done wonders. He'd used that inexhaustible energy to tire Stern out physically—every dare in the book—and then he'd talked Rosa out mentally. Whatever Brain aug she had, she wasn't advertising it, but that didn't stop Ace from asking her fourteen million exhausting questions.

When Stern came back in from the platform, it was thickly dark outside, and he was shaking his head. "Pod came unplugged. It's only half charged. Someone must have tripped over it during our game."

"So we're sleeping here?" Ace yelled. "Amazecraze!" He flicked the gravity lever and rode up into the top bunk like this was camp.

Rosa put on an 8D movie, hoping it would calm Ace down. Little did she know. As soon as the guards were dead asleep in the top bunks, Leo reached up to wake Ace, holding a finger to their lips. Ace slipped down quietly, and Leo lifted themself into their chair with practiced silence. Then they faced the massive storm door.

Ace mouthed *Crap*! without making a sound.

The two of them worked on the door. But even with all Leo's strength, it wouldn't budge more than an inch. Ace found a metal baseball bat, and they used it to pry the door free and wedge it open a few inches. Leo hopped out of their chair and slid sideways through the opening. Ace collapsed the chair and slid it through next. By the time Ace was on the other side, they were already rolling toward the towering shadow of that silver steeple. A curled shell of steel created a nautilus that wound around to the center, sheltering a room of elevators and oddly shaped smaller doors.

"It's like Otis on steroids!" Ace whispered. He loved that AI elevator at ToP.

Leo lifted a small panel to stare at the controls. It displayed the worst possible news: a security scanner that needed a special chip. Sooo easy for Jayla to get around; impossible for everyone else. They slumped back in their chair, feeling dumb in a way that immediately made them want to smash a BESTBall at a wall.

"You made two mistakes." A voice spoke through the darkness.

Ace and Leo turned to find Rosa watching them, arms crossed. "First, you didn't realize that this elevator would have the highest security possible. Second, you didn't figure out my aug."

"WeatherVein," Ace guessed. "Because of all the storms up here. Or maybe PassPort since you've got to guard the entrance and talk to all kinds of people? Not Mimic, otherwise you would have been as good at BESTBall as Leo."

Rosa shook their head once.

"Sherlock," Leo said quietly. "You're a Sherlock."

"Oh, game over." Ace looked suspicious. "Wait, *no one* gets approved to try Sherlock."

"Almost no one. For good reason too." Rosa stared at Leo. "I've deduced that you are searching for a friend. Most likely your fourth boxmate. That much was easy for me, but Aria underestimated you. It's only a matter of time before she heads back up here and demands my assessment on what you three are really up to."

"Us? You're hiding out here in the middle of the Pacific." Leo's voice dared Rosa to explain; the young guard didn't take the dare. All this stuffy secrecy was starting to itch. "What's the Resistance even doing out here?"

"Here's what I *can* say." Rosa glanced at Leo's trilogy of

aug track bracelets. "If you've got your choice of any aug and you go any direction but Brain, you don't deserve to be in Brain."

"Wait, so you're former cadets and you love your augs, but you joined the Resistance anyway?" Ace wondered aloud. "What happened?"

"You're cadets now, but you ran away from ToP."

"That doesn't answer my question." Ace pouted, but Leo thought maybe it did. They'd all signed up for augs. But for Bixonics? That wasn't a team anyone was jumping up and down to join—at least, not in their box.

Rosa pushed her hair from her eyes and squinted at them. Leo swore they could nearly feel her gathering more information, deducing, mapping. Leo should have known better; of course the young guards on the platform were powerful figures in the Resistance.

A Sherlock aug. Whoa. It meant that Rosa's brain could work out just about anyone's motives and plans. Leo had one choice and one choice only. Convince them with the naked truth.

Easier said than done.

"We're searching for Grayson Bix, our boxmate. My . . ." Leo's throat squeezed around the label, making it nearly impossible to voice. "*Best friend.* He went missing hours after his aug surgery. We followed a signal on Jayla's interface, but it disappeared when we got close to this spot and our . . ." Leo glanced at Ace. "Our pilot didn't know to check the power levels, and we ran out of juice."

Ace threw his hands up. "It was my second time flying!"

Leo pushed on. "Jayla got jacked sending out an SOS signal, and then they just hauled her away, and we need to make sure she's okay. And we need to find our boxmate before something happens to him."

It might've been the most they'd ever spoken in their life. They were out of breath from it.

Rosa loved the information. It seemed to feed their aug. They breathed deeply, satisfied. "Everything's coming up Grayson Bix these days. *Game over*, indeed." She reached over to the panel, flipped it up, and let it scan a chip on her sleeve. The first set of heavy titanium doors opened, revealing clear glass doors inside. Then those opened too, and Ace and Leo were looking into the elevator that would bring them down into Atlantis.

"They'll have her in the med center, most likely. Sub-level forty-two. If I were you, I'd come up with a better plan for what to do when you get down there than this 'plan.'"

"You're just . . . helping us?" Ace was confused; Leo wasn't.

"You know why they keep a Sherlock up top, cadets?"

They both shook their heads.

"To figure out who is Resistance and who isn't."

"You think *we're* Resistance?" Ace asked.

"Only time will tell. Time and Sherlock." Rosa snorted

with amusement. Ace stepped into the enormous elevator, as big as the main room in their box. Leo pushed in too and turned on the spot to face the young guard. Rosa continued, "There's one thing that's certain. Never varies in all my predictions. You can't bring down Bixonics without Grayson Bix. He's the key to the whole empire. Especially now."

"What does that mean?" Leo asked.

"You'll figure it out." Rosa motioned for Leo to roll close for a more personal exchange. "Hey, the cost of knowing too little is getting marooned in the ocean."

"Yeah, we've sorted that much," they muttered. "Thanks."

"But what's the cost of knowing too much?"

Leo's mouth froze open and empty. The doors closed on Rosa's smirk and half-veiled eyes as the elevator dropped into the unfathomable depths of the deep blue sea.

Jayla

4

CODE SMELL:
Early problems within a program

[bad news: it worked]

Jayla's network hummed through her. She felt it cycling, cycling, cut off from the satellites and streams of information that fed it, unable to get a signal of any kind. She was tired, but she felt way better.

Even without her eyes open, she knew her aug had left her a message. Little by little, she could read its words in her mind without the interface screen. This was good news for someone with the XConnect aug, although programming was still impossible without an external control to keep track of it all.

Jayla cracked one eye open, confirming all her suspicions. Hospital bed and beeping machines. She must have really overdone it this time, but as long as Leo and Ace were not still in the middle of the ocean cracking desperately at a coconut, this was worth it. She had a vague memory of her mom, and the flight out, and being *really mad* that she hadn't been able to make sure her friends were safe before she was whisked away.

That was the first order of business.

At least this place could not be mistaken for a Bixonics facility. The tree logo of the Resistance was stamped onto the curtain that surrounded her bed. The sight of it—not flickering on a surface at ToP like a secret sign but permanent, welcoming ink—filled her with muddy feelings she'd nearly forgotten about.

The same feelings that had made her run away in the first place.

The Resistance had always been so large in her life, her parents' first baby. She'd drowned in jealousy at the attention it got, but she was too old to have those feelings now, wasn't she? Didn't she go to ToP to *stop* being second violin to the movement?

She was a little stunned to find a window on her left, and beyond it, nothing but deep water and neon glowing specks. This did not help her anxiety at all . . .

[bad news: it worked]

Jayla dropped her head back onto the soft pillow. This was not how she'd always imagined returning home. Not. At. All. Nope, nope, nope.

Familiar voices announced themselves on the other side of the curtain. "*Bad news* could mean anything. No, Aria, listen. The contradiction of something working but also causing negative results could be—"

"It's *bad news* because she doesn't want to be with us, Charlie."

"She sent me a message! To come get her! Haven't you been waiting for this exact moment for over a year and a half?" Jayla's dad's voice was hard to listen to, so warm and familiar, yet so distant in her memories. She'd been away from home for far too long. So long that wherever she was—under the freakin' ocean?—she knew she wasn't home, even if her parents were here.

"It was an emergency code. If she'd had a choice, she wouldn't have sent it to us. You. She messaged *you*, not me," Jayla's mom corrected. "I got to see how displeased she was to see *me* pull up."

Oh, good. They were still arguing over which one of them Jayla liked better. As if that was ever a good idea!

It also seemed that her parents had gone and read her interface while she was unconscious, which was just rude. And completely like them.

Jayla had dreamed about how this moment would turn out in so many different ways. Coming back with all the information she'd gleaned about the corporation, she'd be powerful and in control, with an inside track on the Bix-onics network.

She had always been wearing a truly smashtastic outfit in her daydreams.

But this reality wasn't going to have that kind of

dramatic reveal. Instead, she was all wired up in a bed, wearing a sheet of paper that was supposed to be a nightgown.

She found blankets folded at her waist, pulled them up, and interrupted her parents' argument as if not a single note had changed in all this time apart. "I'm awake. And I'm *fine!*"

Her parents threw back the privacy curtain and nearly ran at her. They didn't look like they had when she'd left them. Older wasn't the right word. They looked . . . tired. Like they'd been awake for many years. They rushed to either side of the bed and each claimed a hand. She could feel how much they loved her. It was a tidal wave of feelings, and Jayla hated getting knocked down by it.

"I'm fine," Jayla said again, although stupid tears were trying to crop up.

"Oh, Jayjay." Her dad came in for a hug, and she squeezed him. Apparently, he was the last person on the planet who could use her baby nickname and not make her feel like a baby. Or maybe she just didn't mind being his baby.

Jayla'd forgotten how shiny his bald brown head appeared under fluorescent lights, or how he had the exact same shade of eyes as her own. He let her go too fast, clearing his throat and clearly trying to go back to *serious mode* so as to create a united front with her mom. "Fine isn't the word I would use, but—"

"Coma," her mom shot in. "*Coma* is the word. You were nearly in a coma."

"I'm here for two minutes after not seeing you for a year and a half, and I get the five-year-old treatment?"

"We're just relieved you're safe," her dad tried, but then he glanced down at the hand he was holding, at the interface blinking as her network tried to connect. He chuckled. "'Bad news,' huh? Bad news that your parents saved your reckless butt?"

Jayla cleared the message. "I'm not explaining if you've already judged me."

Her dad pulled up a chair. Her mom stood even taller. Aria was as put together as ever. She wore a pressed button-down and stiff slacks—like she had to give a speech in front of a lot of people later, but then, didn't she always look that way? Her hair was different at least. Not full, round, and soft but braided back in neat rows, accented with a razor-sharp, zigzagging part. She always looked so cool. She made it seem effortless.

Jayla knew better.

Her mom surprised her by also pulling up a chair. Her parents stared at her for a solid minute before Jayla realized that they were going to let her explain.

"So, Grayson, my boxmate, went missing after his aug surgery. He's one of my best friends. I need to make sure he's okay."

"You were *best friends* with Grayson Bix? We knew you were boxmates, but . . ."

Past tense struck Jayla squarely. Whoa. *Were* best friends? *Were* boxmates?

"Is Grayson dead?" Jayla's fears overloaded her network. She'd programmed the network to meet all strong feelings with immediate options.

[objective: feel better. action plan: Jayla needs the location of Grayson Bix . . . searching . . . searching . . . searching . . .]

Without connectivity, her network was going to zap her energy while it spun for a signal. "Can you unlock whatever's firewalling my network? It's giving me a headache."

"No, we can't unlock *the ocean*," her mom said, motioning to the window. An enormous fish swam by at that exact moment, and Jayla blinked hard. She kept forgetting that she was literally under the sea. How was that possible?

"Where are we?"

Her parents exchanged glances again. Her dad pulled out a device that he waved over her head and the arm bearing the interface. "Still all clear. No tracking signal or control lock detected."

"Of course I'm not sending out a tracker. I wouldn't be that dumb. I erased all the Bixonics training protocols when I left ToP. My network is a free, independent system, governed by only me. I've spent the last year creating it."

"That's not possible." Her dad got too excited, leaning

in. "I've been working on something like that for ages. It's impossible to detangle the aug protocol from the tracking software. When I try to remove one, the other shuts down and the augged person—" He stopped talking because from the look on Jayla's mom's face, he probably should not have said all that. "Well, you're not broadcasting a tracking signal. And that makes you the first cadet we've picked up who isn't."

"Bixonics is tracking all their cadets?" This wasn't new information, but Jayla hadn't thought about it too much before. "Just our locations or how our augs perform? Is the tracker for registration and maintenance?"

Jayla's mom laughed hollowly. "Oh, how easy it is to excuse their human rights violations. Let's track every kid through their aug. That's normal, no problem there."

"You don't know half of what it's like to have an aug."

Or to *not* have an aug in a world of people with augs.

"And you don't know what's it like to have a bio-engineered technological system embedded inside your only child."

Jayla's dad spread out his hands between them. "No fighting. Please."

Jayla and her mom sulked identically. Jayla's network was loud and annoying in her thoughts without connectivity, the wheel of processing spinning and spinning inside her. "Please just let me join whatever service you've got down here. I need to acclimate to this place. Let me have the login codes. Please?"

Her parents exchanged a look that scanned easily without her network's help. It read: *we don't know if we can trust you*.

Now she was angry. "Where are we? Some deepscraper? That's where you've been this whole time? I know I'm the problem child who *ran away*, but at least you knew where I was. You didn't even leave a message, so I'd know you were okay." Every word made Jayla feel younger. In trouble. Upset in a way that made her hands clench. "I didn't know where you were."

"We didn't know if it was safe to get you that message." Her dad's voice pleaded for understanding. And she understood. She understood that the Resistance's needs came before her family's needs. And always had.

It's why she'd run away to ToP to begin with.

"But you knew how to get in contact with us," her mom reminded her with a softer voice. "Isn't that why you're here now? Because you asked for our help, and I came and got you."

"Wait." Jayla sat up. "Where are Leo and Ace?"

"Headed back to ToP. It's important that they know as little as possible about our location and involvement with the Resistance in case they reveal information to the wrong people."

"But I didn't get to say goodbye." Frustration rose in her body like pressure. She ignored her network, which immediately suggested her favorite meditation exercise. "You have no idea what's going on! Dr. Bix might've made Grayson disappear. Or his mom abducted him. Or some other company stole him for leverage! You know loads of shady people have been out for the secret of the Bixonium formula!"

Her parents exchanged sharp glances *again*, and then her dad spoke. "We don't know anything specific about Dr. Bix's intentions for his son, but we're not turning a blind eye to the situation. Trust us."

Well, that was a weird thing to say.

"What *do* you know?" she asked. Jayla's mom made that patented disappointed sound that meant that Jayla was being rude. She amended. "Okay, how about I answer a question, and then you answer one."

Her parents had one of their wordless arguments, and Jayla's dad seemed to come out on top. "Tell us how you became Grayson's boxmate. We were surprised that you would put yourself in that much direct danger. He's constantly monitored by the corporation."

Jayla wanted to skip to the problem. To answers. But she knew her parents too well. They loved facts. Hard intel. They were as hungry for answers as her network. Plus, there was a particular code smell to this exchange—her parents were hiding something—and in programming, the only way out of a problem was to go deeper in.

"I wasn't assigned to Grayson's box right away, but

Dr. Bix padded his son with all these superstar cadets. I showed off, and I got moved up to be with him. I was going to spy on him *for you*, but Grayson's real decent. He is . . . well, he's not like his dad. He didn't even know if he wanted to get an aug, but his . . ."

Her voice trailed off because that part was a bit condemning.

"But his dad made him because he's the poster child for the corporation?" This time Jayla simply nodded at her mom's knowing, judging tone. "What I will tell you, Jayla, is that he is safe. The Resistance saw to it. But that is *all* I will say."

"He's here? Can I see him?"

This time her dad answered. "We took him to be with his mom. It's important that they be together right now, and that we leave them to make their peace."

What did *that* mean? And why did it sound so bad? If something was happening that Grayson had to make peace with, Jayla needed to be there for him. Hands down.

"Okay, my turn." Her dad was so excited all of a sudden and it lightened things. "We've had quite the challenge keeping your signal from accessing the Atlantean network. What you've got there is more powerful than our entire security system."

"I designed it myself." Oh, how Jayla wanted to show her parents what it could do. What *she* could do. She harnessed whatever patience she had and stared straight into her mom's dark brown eyes. "Leo, Ace, and I stole Grayson's hoverpod to look for him. I ended the training protocol on my aug, deleted the firewall, so that we could keep tracking him. We followed his signal out over the water until it vanished."

"That's the satellite blocker. Worth every hour of calculation." Her dad was proud. "Stops all signals from coming in or out of Atlantis. Combine that with the limitations of the ocean, and we've got a Bixonics-free paradise down here in New Atlantis."

"So Grayson is here somewhere too?"

Two things happened next. Jayla learned by their silence that she'd been tracking the helo that had whisked Grayson away and was right to follow it, and two, they weren't going to tell her more. She still didn't have *the clearance* or whatever.

It broke her heart.

"If you deleted the Bixonics systems, you can't go back. They'll consider your aug a rogue liability." Her dad sounded newly worried. He even wrung his hands. "You don't know how hard Bixonics works to recover their lost property. To reclaim augs that aren't being used the way Bixonics wants them to be used."

"I'm not going back to ToP," Jayla said at the same time that her mom said, "You aren't going anywhere." And even though they'd technically agreed, Jayla gritted her teeth in frustration. "I am trying to tell you that. I'm back. With you. To help."

Please be happy about that.

[objective: feel better. action plan: Jayla needs to feel welcome. searching . . . searching . . . searching . . .]

She crossed her arms so that her parents couldn't see her network trying to stitch up her cracked heart. She was *here*. Right here in front of them, and yet she'd never felt further away. "I have all sorts of new intel to share. A whole new perspective to bring to the Resistance's work!"

Jayla had learned the hard way at a young age that she couldn't compete with the importance and magnitude of the Resistance when it came to her parents. Her mom literally started the movement from her basement and her dad had been one of the first surgeons at ToP before his change of heart. Aria had whisked him away in the dead of night in a helo, just like Grayson. And then they'd fallen in love. And Jayla was born.

And *this* was why Jayla had gone to ToP, to get an aug that would help the Resistance. To be important to the movement and show her parents that she was the best of both of them, all in one stylish person. Only when she looked at them now, she knew that's not what they saw. They saw a young person who'd spent the last eighteen months probably being brainwashed by Bixonics.

What she wouldn't give for Leo or Gray . . . or even wild-hearted Ace to be here. She was stronger with her boxmates by her side. She needed to be stronger to unpack all that had happened over the last few days.

[objective: feel better. action plan: find friends. scanning . . . scanning . . . bio match for Ace and Leo on sublevel seventy-four . . .]

Headed back to ToP. Her mom's words hung in her mind crookedly. Jayla's feelings created a standoff as she glanced at her interface. Leo and Ace *were* still here somewhere. Were they up to their sneaky, unstoppable ways without her?

Or were her parents lying?

5

COWBOY:
A hacker without patience

[connectivity: offline]

No matter what Jayla tried, she could not get onto the Atlantean network, and without it, the surrounding ocean and her dad's prized surface satellite blocker truly did dampen any access to the fantastic limitless information streaming topside. It was sort of genius to have a Resistance base down here, in a purely irritating way.

Jayla paced the small medical room. Her parents had left for an urgent meeting—to discuss what to do about her sudden arrival and untethered aug, most likely. Ordinarily, she'd have been annoyed that they'd kept her here under the pretext that she might not be well, even though her network had let her know hours before that she was fine. The doctors had treated her aug like a suspicious virus and wouldn't accept any of its bioscans.

Jayla got dressed and stood in front of the huge window

that looked out into the dark ocean. Fish and algae had collected around the lights of the deepscraper windows, creating a vertical shaft of marine life that shouldn't exist in the blackest part of the sea. It was pretty cool, but Jayla had bigger fish to fry.

She peeked out around the curtain at the medical bays on this level. Everyone was so busy that she was able to sneak from curtain to curtain, following the signs for the elevators. Right before she made it to the exit, an entire unit of nurses and doctors and medbots turned a corner, headed her way fast, and she had no choice but to duck inside the nearest bay.

She tucked the curtain around her and froze as the footsteps drilled by. Her dad's most serious voice passed, giving medical orders, followed by the squeaking tracks of a bot that needed to be serviced.

It wasn't until they were gone that she turned and found the bed in this bay occupied.

Amir was squinting at her. He sat cross-legged on the mattress, and when she went to say something, he held up a hand to stop her. His mouth moved with unspoken calculations, his eyes glazed. He was writing code. Right there, without his interface. And she'd been wrong, he wasn't squinting at her so much as peering into the back of his own mind, using his XConnect without his interface.

Jayla was fascinated. She'd heard of people with their aug being able to do this—heard that Amir could—but she'd never seen it before. Amir had been the grad aug who'd helped her those first few weeks after her surgery. He'd been sort of kind, sort of short-tempered, as he drilled her on writing basic software, creating balloons and other elementary images from scratch in the hololab. It felt like a lifetime ago, even though it had been only a few months.

He even looked different. His brown skin was paler under the fake light and his green eyes were distant. His hair was all fluffed and sticking up all over the place, making him seem less intimidating for once. When Amir finished, he blinked hard and stared at her. The interface on his arm that matched Jayla's was covered by a thick bandage.

"What are you doing here?" she blurted.

"Same question. You first."

Well, Jayla wasn't going to answer that. She was pretty sure her parents hadn't advertised that they had a runaway child at ToP. Maybe no one here even knew who she was. That could work in her favor. "I got rescued by the Resistance. Duh."

"Well, I work for the Resistance. And you're not supposed to be here." He spoke English with an Arabic accent. Jayla had dug that about him when he was helping her back at ToP. "Do your parents know that you're walking around off the cadet level?"

Cadet level?

"You know who my parents are?" she asked. He arched

one eyebrow in response. Maybe her parents *hadn't* hidden their relationship with her. But that just introduced a new question. "You weren't spying on me for them at ToP, were you?"

"Spy? No. Sentry? Yes." Amir kicked his legs down from the bed and stood. "You have no idea how hard it was to protect your boxmates from their own overwhelming curiosity." He stretched, wincing when he lifted his bandaged arm over his head.

"What's wrong with your interface?"

"I had it removed."

"You've *lost* your XConnect?" Jayla felt that in the gut. Despite everything she believed about Bixonics and the Resistance, she loved her network, her aug. Loved the power it gave her and direction it brought to her life.

To lose it or risk it . . .

"I don't need the interface to use my aug, so I had your dad take it out. Bixonics tracks their hardware to the ends of the earth. Surely you know that already. They're tracking every single cadet they aug."

She wasn't sure what she knew, apart from being annoyed at Amir's know-it-all tone. "Well, not me."

"That's not possible."

Jayla was done with this conversation. She craned her neck around the curtain and found a clear path to the elevators. "I'm capable of impossible. Deal with it."

She left, jogging to the elevators. Once there, she

found out fast that the entire system was controlled by a password chip of some kind. She could hack into it, but it would take time without a login to the Atlantean network.

Amir followed her, shaking his head as her attention flicked from the access panel to her interface. She wrote a quick, sloppy code that would hopefully override the security, call the elevator, and bring her to Ace and Leo. "All right, cowboy. Slow down with the hacking for a sec. I've got a hall pass. Where are you headed?"

Jayla scowled at him. It *would* be a lot faster if he helped. "Seventy-four."

Amir reached over and called the elevator with an access chip on his sleeve. "Cadet level. I'll come with you."

Over the next few minutes, Jayla learned a lot about the Resistance. This was more than a deepscraper base where her parents ran secret countermeasures against the Bixonics's ever-spreading empire. It was a place where lots of families lived. An entire underwater city. The sublevel selections on the elevator screen proved it. There were listings for everything from a gelato shop to a mall to a preschool and a walk-in clinic.

Sublevel seventy-four was listed simply as *Restricted*.

What in the world were Leo and Ace doing there?

Amir kept a trained eye on her, and she kept ignoring him. Had he really been *watching* her in his role as a grad aug? That would make him a ToP double agent, and that was *her* idea. And *her* role in the Resistance.

When the elevator doors opened, she walked out like she knew where she was going, which of course she didn't. She didn't make it far. The elevator doors left her on a balcony overlooking a room as cavernous as the Coliseum at ToP. One end of the space held an enormous, indoor arena where hundreds of young people ran through an elaborate obstacle course, similar to the training equipment at ToP. The other side seemed to be a food court, and maybe Jayla was imagining it, but there appeared to be rows and rows of bunk beds stacked ten high at the farthest end.

"What am I looking at?" she breathed.

"A sanctuary for in-between souls," Amir said, leaning on the balcony beside her. The mezzanine level wrapped all the way around this level, creating a 360-degree bird's-eye view of the place. "This is where we bring the cadets who want out of the B.E.S.T. Program. After a person has gotten an aug, they're technically property of Bixonics Corp. This is the only available freedom for them. A secret hideaway where they can start new lives, free of Bixonics reclamation workers."

If that was true, what were Leo and Ace doing here? Neither of them had had their aug surgeries yet. Neither of them had even picked an aug.

Jayla keyed in a few commands on her interface until she could pinpoint exactly where Leo's and Ace's bioscans were coming from in this mess of hundreds of cadets. Had her parents dumped them here after they rescued her?

Was that why they had been so cagey on the med level? "I've got things to do. You can go away." She paused for a second and looked at him. "You don't have to *spy* on me anymore."

She walked away, and he didn't follow this time.

Jayla trailed the signal on her interface around the mezzanine to a ramp that wound down to the main floor. She blended into the crowd so easily. Everyone was about her age. This was wild. She jogged toward the signal for Ace and Leo and found them tucked away behind a mountain of linens. Ace was just about to climb into what looked like an automated laundry chute.

"Wait! Stop!"

Leo whipped their head around at the sound of Jayla's voice. The three boxmates collapsed into a quick hug of reunion.

"You're all right?" Leo asked nervously. "We were worried."

"Yeah, my parents are being overprotective, but I'm good. This place, though . . ."

Ace bounced on the balls of his feet. "It's so much more than a secret base, Jayla! People live here. Like when these cadets grow up, they stay here, in New Atlantis. People get married and have kids and careers and stuff! They say they'll never go topside again!"

"Because Bixonics will reclaim them," Leo added coldly.

Something heavy dropped in Jayla's stomach. She sort

of wished she'd been kinder to Amir and gotten more answers from him. "How'd you both get down here? My parents assured me you were headed back to ToP."

"Leo sweet-talked the guards on the surface so we could pop down here and check on you and keep looking for Gray. We nearly made it to the med level, but then some Resistance people found us and brought us here, thinking we'd just gone wandering without permission."

"Gray's not here." Leo's voice was small but certain. "No one has seen him, and you know he doesn't go unnoticed anywhere. Have you found his signal at all?"

She shook her head. "Just the two of you. It's like he's vanished."

Jayla did not know how to tell her friends that her parents knew where Grayson was, but they weren't sharing the info. "The Resistance is having an emergency meeting, trying to figure out what to do with me. Apparently, it's very confusing that my aug has been untethered from the Bixonics system. We need to get both of you out of here before they won't let you leave. They're already paranoid that you know too much."

"They think we'll tattle?" Ace asked. "Are they going to wipe our memories?"

"They can't do that," Jayla said, while Leo added, "Too many movies, Ace."

Jayla led the boxmates back toward the elevators where Amir was still hanging out. This time, she tried smiling at him. He arched one of those thick, dark eyebrows at her.

"Hey, Amir! What're you doing here?"

Amir looked at the two rogue cadets with a stunned expression. "They're not supposed to be here."

"You've got to get some new material," Jayla said. "Mind using your little chip there to give us a lift to the surface?"

He shook his head. "No one gets out. These elevators are programmed to not allow it." She sighed hard. How could someone so accomplished with their XConnect not know how to reprogram something like this? Before she could respond, he held up a hand to stop her words. "But I know another way."

HACK:
Get sneaky and proactive

Amir used the chip he called his "hall pass" to take the boxmates to the bottom floor of the deepscraper, sublevel one hundred.

"How come we can't feel the water pressure at this depth?" Ace asked.

"This whole place is pressurized," Amir elaborated. "Like a submarine."

"As if we need to be under any more pressure," Leo muttered just loud enough for Jayla to hear, who snorted.

She found herself asking her network for the blueprints to Atlantis—curious about its construction and the renovations that had made it into this Resistance stronghold—before she remembered that her network couldn't do much more than monitor her thoughts and body. She'd even turned it on low-power mode while connectivity was down.

Being without her aug made her feel little again. Little and powerless. She hated it.

How had her parents even created this place? Turned it into this? Not even a year and a half ago, her mom had been running meetings out of their attic and her dad had a lab in the basement. Now they had a . . . city.

Amir slid into a whole speech about how the pressurization worked and the new meds pumped into the atmosphere to keep everyone from getting the bends in the elevator and whatnot, but Jayla was distracted. This was a different kind of level than any other she'd seen so far in Atlantis: an entire open floor where submersibles were lined up in a circle around the outer wall, each one with their own water lock launching bay.

"Is this a little army or something?" she asked.

"They're tendersubs. Lifeboats. Or life-subs. In case there's an emergency, and we all have to abandon deep-scraper."

To Jayla's shock, he walked to the nearest one, pressed a button, and the front of the tendersub opened with a slight mechanical whine. Amir climbed into the pilot's chair and Ace was right behind him.

Jayla planted her feet. "How is going into the ocean going to help them get to their hoverpod on the surface?"

"You'll see." Amir beckoned for them to follow.

Ace yelled, "This is epic!"

Leo hopped down from their chair and climbed in. Still skeptical, Jayla collapsed Leo's chair and stored it, then sat in the front while Amir strapped into the pilot's seat.

With a practiced air, Amir closed the hatch and opened the water lock door, sending the tender down a track to wait in the interim space between ocean and Atlantis proper. He flipped another switch, the door shut behind them, and the cramped space filled with water.

Jayla watched the ocean stream in all around the outside of the tender. The long, narrow front window was obviously many, many inches thick to withstand the pressure, but her heart still hammered. This was exciting. No, it was foolish. Foolish *and* exciting. Her network woke up, even though she'd put it in low-power mode.

[objective: deal with anxious excitement. action plan: happy soundtrack. play now?]

Jayla shook her head once, and her network gave up suggesting smooth jazz or meditation. She needed to trust Amir, and that wasn't something she was good at or something that her network could help her with. Also, there was this pesky, brand-new issue of her parents. If they found out she'd escaped again, they'd be hurt. Jayla didn't want to keep hurting them, and yet, she couldn't just sit here while Gray was in the middle of something that was bad enough to worry her parents. She couldn't just sit here while cadets not unlike Leo and Ace were adjusting to having *an entire life* underwater. They deserved freedom. All of them.

Why her parents didn't understand *that* was starting to hurt Jayla.

"Will anyone know we busted out?" she asked.

"People take the tenders out all the time. They're not supposed to, but they're also not supposed to go unused either. Bad for the fuel cells. They definitely won't think it's a couple of teenagers out for a joyride."

This was the first time Jayla had *ever* been called a teenager, and technically she wouldn't be thirteen for a few more weeks, but she loved it.

Jayla leaned forward to look through the window. The water lock seemed full. "What happens next?"

Amir waved his hand over a blue button like a magician. "Who wants to press eject?"

"I do!" Ace shot forward between them and whacked the button. The doors between the water lock and the Pacific Ocean opened slowly. She didn't know what to expect, but the water was dark here. Like staring into a night sky without any stars. "It's not much of a view."

"Just wait."

The submersible released into the open water, moving forward very slowly.

Jayla gripped her armrests while Amir used the steering console to turn the tender 180 degrees so that they were facing up the side of the deepscraper. Ace gasped, Jayla cursed, Amir chuckled. Leo was as silent as ever. From the outside, Atlantis was a work of beauty. The one hundred sublevels beneath the surface created a magnificent tower of light not unlike the holiday lights on ToP this time of year.

Algae and other marine life swam, hovered, and grew around all the windows, thriving at unusual depths because of the grow lights shining out into the endless dark.

"How'd they turn this deepscraper into a Resistance base?" Ace asked, looking out the window. "We're literally in the midnight zone!"

"They moved down here when I was at ToP. They don't trust me enough to tell me yet," Jayla admitted, and that stung, didn't it? "The Resistance has always thrived on being secretly against Bixonics. Helping people who find themselves on the recalled side of the corporation. Amir could probably tell you more," she added without a pointed edge. "Now they can just keep on whisking cadets away in the middle of the night. Plenty of room down here."

Leo spoke suddenly. "They *did* steal Grayson away, didn't they?"

Jayla stared at Amir, knowing that he could say for sure. "They said he's with his mom, but also they were weird, like something bad is going on and Gray's in the middle of it. Believe me, they are not going to tell us. They think we're Team Bixonics."

Ace looked like he was about to argue that he *was* Team Bixonics, but Leo's gruff, quiet voice beat him to it. "Everything's coming up Grayson Bix," they murmured.

Amir looked over his shoulder at them, and Jayla did too. "What's that?" she asked.

"Just something I heard. Seems important."

Great. Now even Leo was being cagey.

Amir turned the tender back toward the open water and dialed up the speed. Jayla could feel the submersible's movement in her body, even if the view out the window remained unchanged. There was even a slight incline; they were moving toward the surface.

Jayla relaxed as they climbed ever so slowly up.

Amir played with the steering console. All the while, the ocean around them brightened like a slow, clear sunrise, changing from black to navy, navy to cobalt, cobalt to indigo, indigo to baby blue. Jayla was so surprised when she saw the surface, she gasped when they broke through, the water parting like crystal curtains.

[connectivity: offline. satellite network blocked.]

The little tendersub slid onto the sand of a small beach beneath a towering silver steeple covered in the canopy that must have been the satellite blocker her dad was so proud of. Jayla's heart hammered suddenly. She *did not* want to get caught out here, running off again after having finally come back to them.

Instead of opening the hatch, Amir turned to face Leo

and Ace. "Be careful. Trust no one."

"Can we talk to you if we see you on campus?" Ace asked.

"I won't be going back again." He glanced at the arm that used to have his interface, and then at Jayla for some reason. Amir was sad to not be able to go back; she felt the sting of it too. They both had no choice but to find some way forward.

Amir opened the hatch, and Ace went out first, bringing Leo's chair all the way to where Grayson's hoverpod sat. Watching him go filled Jayla with tough feelings. There was no sign of the guards Ace had talked about nonstop, the ones called Rosa and Stern. Perhaps they were asleep. It did look like five in the morning up here. Was that why Jayla was nearly nodding off?

Leo hugged Jayla fiercely. "He's not gone," they whispered. "Promise me that."

"We aren't giving up." Jayla stared at Leo, holding their shoulders. "We will find out what's happening to Grayson Bix. And that means spying on *both* sides."

Leo nodded as if they already had some grand plan.

"I'll get you a message as soon as I know more. Be on the lookout for it."

Ace ran back to say goodbye, and all of a sudden, Jayla was watching her boxmates fly away in Grayson's hoverpod, headed back to the life she was letting go of.

She glanced at Amir. He had this habit of watching

her; she remembered it from their post-surgery lessons when her aug was an alien inside her brain that she kept trying to coax out. That didn't explain why he was still doing it now. "What?"

"You really aren't transmitting an aug tracker, are you?"

Oh, that was the look. He was scanning her with his own XConnect. She had to admit that he was much slyer without needing the interface to organize things. "I'll teach you how I did it if you show me how to use my aug without the interface."

The hoverpod was nearly out of sight now. They both squinted at it. Maybe they both wished they were on it.

"Deal," Amir said without looking at her.

GRAYSON

INTERLUDE

The small room Grayson Bix had woken up in following surgery—the one with the fake windows and deep-sea vibes—was in the center of a circular hotel suite.

At least, it felt like one of those fancy hotels his dad used to take his family to when he was little and they were still one unit. Before the divorce. And his mom's sudden and complete disappearance. There was always some outstanding feature, like ice walls or an indoor waterfall.

Here the outer walls were all glass, with a 360-degree view of the black bottom of the ocean. It was beautiful and cold—and there was a lot of medical equipment. What was this place? And why was he *all alone*?

Grayson nearly stumbled when his turn around the suite ended in an open living room area where someone was sleeping on the couch, curled up in a comfy blanket. He ran to her, couldn't stop himself, and threw his arms around her before realizing that she was hooked to a lot of machines and was thinner than she'd ever been his whole life.

But that barely mattered because she was *real*.

"Mom," he whispered, waking her slowly, a careful hand on her shoulder.

She sat up, blinked back the confusion of sleep, and shouted with joy.

They embraced for long minutes, rocking and crying.

"Oh, my baby," she said into his neck, hugging him tightly. She was as thin as a bird in Grayson's arms. "They promised they'd get you here before it was too late."

LEVEL TWO:

LEO

7

SIDELINED:
Forced out of the action

Leo had never felt so driven, even though they were stuck in their bedroom at home.

Ever since meeting the mysterious, eclectic guard in New Atlantis, they could not stop thinking about the Sherlock aug. Or more specifically, they couldn't stop remembering the way Rosa had been mapping possible futures, labeling Grayson *the key* to sorting out the corporation turned empire known as Bixonics.

Leo needed to see those possible futures as well. It was the only way they'd be able to help Gray. They scrolled through the Bixonics website's information on Sherlock, but the six sentences said nothing beyond marketing the aug:

Do you . . . SHERLOCK? Know more, know faster. Become the solution with an aug that turns your brain into your very own mind palace. Cadets approved for the

Sherlock trial aug will undergo rigorous mental training. Cadets approved to become one of the planet's elite Sherlockians must pass a personality screening. Do you have what it takes to know everything?

Personality screening. This was the only aug with *that* language.

What did it mean?

Leo tapped around on their tablet, but that was all the available information. The description didn't even acknowledge that only *three* people had ever been approved for the Sherlock aug in the entire history of the B.E.S.T. Program. Naturally, Leo had spent the holiday break between semesters tracking them down. One was—obviously—the president of the United States, and there was her picture right there. The other was Rosa. And then there was a missing Sherlock, someone who had been scrubbed from the records . . . which was why Leo was planning to call in an expert. They checked the clock. Two minutes.

Leo closed out the screen and flicked up the image of a tropical mountain. It filled their bedroom with warm greens and jungle sounds. Leo was supposed to be in Fiji. That's where Grayson had wanted to go with Leo to celebrate getting augged and graduating from ToP. They'd been planning the trip for months, and Leo had even gotten permission to miss their family vacation, which they'd forgotten about in all the madness of Gray's disappearance and their desperate rescue mission.

Leo's timer went off and they switched the tablet from projection to streaming video, then placed a call to Ace.

"Hi!" A bright, cheery Ace lookalike in mom form was smiling into the camera. "Hi! You're Leo calling for Ace? He has told us all about—"

"*Mom*!" Ace scurried toward the screen and pulled it out of her hand. Leo fought feeling seasick as Ace ran down a hallway, swinging the tablet, and slammed the door to his room. He hopped onto his bed, rotating the camera around in a way that let them see a pile of superhero costumes and all his Bixonics paraphernalia.

Gray had guessed that Ace was a Bix fanboy upon first meeting . . . but Gray had no idea how deep this ran. Leo had a sudden weird thought . . . could they trust Ace?

They pushed the feeling down, but not away. Everyone—Bixonics, the Resistance, adults in general—always seemed to be doing the right things for the wrong reasons or vice versa. Leo was starting to believe that they'd never know who to trust or how to help Grayson, which brought them straight back to Sherlock.

If Leo had that aug, they'd know. Just like Rosa had *known*.

"Ace!" Leo called out. "Stop moving. The bouncing is going to make me puke."

"Oh yeah, sorry." Ace settled on his bed. "How are you? Are you in trouble for missing the last days of the semester? I'm not. I told them my boxmate gave me a hoverpod because, well, he's Grayson Bix and he can give presents like that. I swear Finn exploded with jealousy. Mama Jay said I had to get a license before I take it up again, but they have a license, so we've already gone for a few joyrides. I saw the Grand Canyon yesterday!"

Leo grinned even though they had to find a way to reach him. "Ace. Bring it in." They sounded like they were back on the court, and it made them think of Gray. Could he watch their BESTBall games from wherever he was being hidden or kept? Could they get a sign to him that way? "Have you heard from Jayla?"

"Nothing, but I think that's a good sign." Ace bounced and then paused, lowering his voice to a whisper. "Finn didn't tell my parents anything. And I broke his nose! He said he tripped. I don't know why he's lying for me, but what's that saying? 'Don't kick a horse in the mouth'?"

Leo snorted but didn't correct him. "Maybe he's embarrassed that you stood up to him."

"He's giving me space. Even Mom thinks it's odd. He's not home now. He went to do something for Dr. Bix. Publicity for TurboLegs, or something. He's in *Tokyo*."

Even after all their questions about who they could trust, Ace still said *Dr. Bix* reverently. Years ago, the famous scientist had introduced himself to Leo as Lance, which they'd never called him. He was always going to be Gray's dad.

"Were your parents suspicious?" Ace asked.

"Only Emma, but she isn't talking to me much. But that's normal." Leo drilled their fingers for a few seconds. "Ace, I need your help. I'm trying to figure out my aug choices."

"Of course you are! Rising third semester. Time for the big decision and to schedule your aug surgery. Wow. Well, I'm glad you came to me. Let's talk Bod first. I'm thinking Hercules could be amazing for—"

"Ace, I'm going Brain."

"For realz? Why?" He exhaled hard. "Okay, okay. Not everyone can be Bod. Are you thinking PassPort? What about Mimic? You'd be unstoppable."

"I've been doing research on Sherlock."

Ace was silent on the other end for a string of moments. Leo thought that if they had Sherlock, they'd know what he was thinking. They'd know all the things, and they wouldn't have to find a way to speak up or ask. Just like Rosa had taken one look at the cadets and known that they were completely up to something.

Ace chewed his lip. "That's not a real choice. They don't ever approve people for that. Only like *really* special people. Like presidents. Or really *the* president."

"And Rosa. I'm triple tracked by Vaughn himself. I already am special."

"Yeah, but didn't he tell you not to do Sherlock? Didn't he kinda promise that you wouldn't get approved for it?"

"Vaughn said it was a waste of a semester, which isn't the same thing." Leo hadn't expected this much resistance from aug-happy Ace. "I need to know what you have on that aug. Who was the third person approved for it, other than the president and Rosa? There's no record online." Ace shrugged. "Can you look into it?"

"Course. I've got my almanac of ToP grads right here. I had to bump the database offline a while ago because it was updating itself like crazy and taking up all the bandwidth in the house, and I swear it was changing old listings. Rewriting the past." Only Ace could say something like that with zero suspicion in his voice.

"Aren't you at all curious why it's being revised?"

"Probably has reasons! Staying accurate, I bet." Ace's parents hollered in the background, and he shouted, "Gotta go. See you Thursday!"

Leo didn't buy that the almanac was keeping up to date. In truth, they were starting to doubt everything Bixonics . . . and Resistance. Maybe all the adults were lying. Leo felt sidelined, as if they'd lost their temper on the court and gotten stuck on the bench by Coach Vaughn to cool off.

Once they had Sherlock, that wouldn't happen again. They'd see it coming.

Leo put the tablet away, bummed that Ace hadn't been more excited by their new direction in augs. Why did everyone sort of turn around when they asked about Sherlock? They wished they could hop back in Gray's hoverpod and ask Rosa a thousand more questions. No. Leo wished they could roll into Gray's room across the hallway in their box and ask him what he knew.

They called up a muted video of Gray and Leo sitting side by side on the couch in their box, playing video games, elbowing each other to gain an upper hand. Months ago, Leo'd started having sort of . . . warm feelings about Gray, but he didn't feel them back, so that was that. They were still friends, and *that* was everything.

Wasn't it?

"Did you two break up?" Emma was standing in Leo's door, having cracked it open to spy on them. Like usual. "You're all upset, and I know you didn't go to any of your classes the last week of the semester. I have reliable sources."

"Gray got his aug and took off to live with his mom." This was the approved story. The one Dr. Bix himself had put out there in the days following Gray's sudden disappearance. Leo knew better; that wasn't even half the story. "I miss him."

"You two were fighting at the dance. Don't think that all these pieces don't add up. I might not be a genius like you and Jayla, but I know a crush gone wrong when I see one."

Leo surprised themself by not being offended for

once by Emma's pushy nosiness. Emma *was* clever. She'd started her own gossip feed at ToP and now she was sort of an authority on all social events at the program. Maybe she knew about the Sherlock aug. Leo opened their mouth to ask, but she spoke first.

"Mom made *your* favorite, so you have to come out of your room for five minutes. You can't hide from everyone forever." Emma turned coldly and left.

Leo rolled out after her, gliding down the long hallway with an exact, practiced push to their wheels. They always shot through this section of the house. Years ago, when Leo had worked up the courage to tell their sister about being nonbinary, Emma had run off to tell their parents, and Leo had found that coming out was as easy as putting Emma in charge. Their parents had been upside down about it for a hot minute, asking things like, *Do you need new clothes?* Which was, of course, *yes*. Whoever had thought up the idea of dressing twins to match was a demented person for sure.

But Leo hadn't spoken up about the pictures in the hallway. The ones of Emma and Leo, frozen in toddlerhood in matching denim jumpers and ponytails. No one knew Leo hated them, so no one took them down.

When Leo was at ToP, they didn't have to think about any of the old, silent pieces of themself. They had Gray, and Jayla, and now Ace. They had Coach Vaughn and

BESTBall and three aug tracks to choose from.

But at home? They were still hiding from their own face on the wall.

No matter what, they were excited to head back to the Tower of Power.

8

SPARRING PARTNER:
Practice fighting with frenemies

Move-in day for Leo's third semester took forever, but finally, they were on the Hyperloop, watching the country blur by the window at breakneck speed.

Leo was alone in the back of the train car. Some idiot cadets from Ace's class had filled the disabled spot with their luggage, and then Emma had made a whole loud ruckus about making them move their stuff when Leo had wheeled in and stared at the only spot for their chair, full of bags. Which was bad enough, but then the cadets started apologizing over and over, and Leo wished they'd had a BESTBall to throw so hard that the self-centered babies were bowled out of the car like in a cartoon.

Leo didn't have any problem with able-bodied people; Leo had a big problem with able-bodied people acting like they were the center of the universe.

After standing up for Leo for the umpteenth time in

their twin life, Emma settled herself on the far side of the car, exhausted and put out. This was the first semester that their parents had let them head back to the program unsupervised. Leo hadn't even had to ask for it; Emma had *insisted* that they be allowed to go alone. There had been a fight in the kitchen. Leo'd heard raised voices and kept to their room until it was over.

The mystery of Emma's newfound independence solved itself when, at the next stop, a tall cadet who had spiky black hair, brown skin, and dimples that deepened at the sight of Emma got on. Leo recognized him from the basketball team. Tosh.

Emma had a secret boyfriend.

They sat snuggled hip to hip. Leo watched as Tosh handed over an earbud so they could sync up and listen to music together. Emma seemed so happy. Leo had sort of forgotten what that expression looked like on their twin's face. Was it even possible that Emma was being boiled in ridiculous feelings all the time as well? Couldn't be true. Emma always seemed okay; it's what she worked hardest at.

Emma glanced over and caught Leo staring. When the Hyperloop sneezed to a stop before ToP and they all piled up to head out the doors, Emma hissed, "Don't tell our parents."

"I didn't say anything."

"You never do." Emma's face was a storm cloud, all

glowering and threatening. "You make me talk and then you don't even say thanks." She pushed her way out. "No wonder Grayson Bix is done with you. I can't wait until you're in your box, and I'm in mine, and we can just . . . pretend we don't know each other."

Leo rocked back on their wheels, feeling a bit punched.

Tosh and Emma walked out holding hands like it was *nothing*. Leo couldn't stop thinking of all the times Gray's and Leo's hands would sort of brush when they were palling around, and then they'd both move away. Like magnets set to repel.

Leo zoomed across the jeweled courtyard of ToP, outstripping most of the cadets easily. Ads flashed under their wheels. At one point, an enormous image of Grayson filled twenty tiles beneath them all at once, and they nearly skidded sideways, trying not to roll over his way-larger-than-life mouth.

Wait.

That was a new ad. Gray had his augged eyes in it! They were the same beautiful brown but with something silver flashing just beneath. Which meant that wherever Gray was with his mom, Bixonics was still positioning him as the company poster boy.

Leo tucked that information away to discuss with Ace ASAP, only by the time they'd made it to Otis, the wild-card elevator, and up to Lilliput in one piece, their beloved box home was ground zero for complete chaos.

Ace was yelling, walking back and forth and waving his arms. And . . . for some reason . . . Siff was kicking back on their sofa, staring at Ace like his fellow second semester had lost his mind.

"What's going on?" Leo rolled in and came to a pointed, sharp stop.

"Hey, boxmate." Siff saluted, two fingers pressed to his blond hair.

Ace pointed at Siff as if those two words explained all the chaos in the entire world.

"Siff is our new boxmate?" Leo squinted at Ace. And then Siff.

"We can't accept this. He is my *archnemesis*!"

"I think that's in your head." Siff put his feet up on the coffee table. "Honestly, being friends with me could be good for you."

"It's obvious, isn't it? He's been sent to spy on us!" Ace started pacing again. "There's no other explanation!"

"Maybe I'm here because I asked to take Gray's room. Have you seen it? It's twice the size of a regular room."

Leo weighed both of their points. "Ace, he's probably just—"

Ace shot into his room and slammed the door. Siff chuckled.

"Don't enjoy his distress too much," Leo managed. "Or you'll really seem like a villain."

Siff stood up and crossed the room. "Got my trial surgery moved up to this semester. Got to rest."

"Just . . . keep out of his way until he's used to you. Okay?"

"For you? Course." He bumped fists with Leo and entered Gray's room like it had always belonged to him. When the door shut, Leo could not help but feel smacked by the words on the digital plaque, woken up by the slamming door. **SIFF, SECOND SEMESTER, HE/HIM**

Somehow that made Gray's absence louder than everything else.

Leo went to Ace's room and did their best to soothe his fears, but he really did have a problem with Siff being one wall away. "He bullied me, Leo. He's a bully. He shut me up in the escape room. It was terrible."

"He won't bully you when I'm around." Leo thought that sounded good, but even they could hear the remaining problem. Leo couldn't be everywhere, especially with BESTBall season starting up soon. "Maybe you'll be a good influence on him."

"*Ugh*, you sound like my moms." Leo stuck out a tongue at him. Ace picked at his blanket. "Before you get *too* comfortable, you should see who is in Jayla's old room." Leo did not like the sound of that, but before they could go check it out, Ace called out. "Wait. I found out the third person with Sherlock. His name is Felix Danvers.

He was in the very first class of cadets. Coach Vaughn's class. Maybe you can get more information from him."

"Wouldn't that mean that there were two Sherlocks in that first class? This Felix *and* the president?"

"Maybe it didn't start out as an impossible aug to get. Maybe that happened later because of that first class. Vaughn's class. We could ask him. Maybe something happened." Ace did this sometimes, said something so smart that Leo marveled at how so many people could underestimate him just because his focus pinged to new subjects at Hyperloop speed.

"Thanks for looking into it." Leo was about to leave but they could tell that Ace was sitting on something bigger than the name *Felix Danvers*. They tucked that bit away to ask Vaughn about later. "What is it?"

"Rosa is sort of dead."

"Rosa?" Leo's jaw dropped open. "How do you know? What happened?"

"Yeah, no. Rosa is listed as dead in my almanac. It says they died two months after they graduated from B.E.S.T., but obviously when we met them, they were alive, so . . ."

"They faked their own death?"

"Looks that way."

"*Whoa*."

"Leo?" Ace shifted on his bed. "Please don't go for that aug. Jayla and Gray are gone. Seems like a recipe for disaster. I don't know what I'd do if something happened to you. This all seems . . . dangerous now."

Leo felt warm. Like maybe they should hug skinny, adorable Ace. They didn't. Their voice shrunk in volume but grew sure of itself. "I'll make you three promises. One, I'm here for you. Two, I'm winning the BESTBall championship this year, and three, no matter what aug I get, we're using it to help . . ." They remembered a little late that they were back on campus and Bixonics was always listening.

"It's okay," Ace said. "I told Otis to block our box from the security feed."

"How do you know it's working?"

"I don't. It's just, I trust Otis. And we got to have some trust here. My moms say that if there's no trust, there's nothing."

Leo couldn't help but agree. "Three, we're going to help *him*. Did you see that new ad in the courtyard? Gray might be out of ToP, but they're still making him do their marketing. I have a bad feeling about it."

Ace nodded, and Leo wheeled out and straight across the common room. Jayla's door was open, and every soft, vibrant, beautiful Jayla item gone. The room was empty. Most likely because a newk was destined for this spot. Leo realized that this would make them the senior cadet in the box, and they weren't wild about having to be in charge. That was Gray's job. Or Jayla's. But certainly not Leo's.

They tapped on the blank digital pad on the door, hoping to at least get a heads-up on a name and pronoun. It wasn't too long ago that Leo had sat on that very common room sofa with Grayson, debating whether *Ace Wells* was going to be as much trouble as Finnegan Wells had been.

The digital plaque on the door flicked on, only it didn't list first semester, but third. And it had *their* name on it. No, not their first name. Their last name.

Otis dinged, opened its doors, and Leo swiveled to face Emma. Tears were streaming down her face, like she'd been screaming into a pillow. All her belongings bobbed in behind her in matching meowing, kitten-faced luggage.

"Don't even look at me, Leo! This is all *your* fault."

Emma pushed passed her twin and slammed the door to her new room. Jayla's room. Emma was their new box-mate? *Emma*? Who'd decided that one? Dr. Bix? There were too many questions. Suddenly it *did* feel like maybe they were being spied on . . . or being kept busy for their own good. Ace would have a hard time focusing with Siff next door, and Emma would have the exact same effect on Leo. Like built-in sparring partners.

Leo went to their room and shut the door. The dark place was full of vampire smiles and BESTBall gear. It smelled like last semester. One of Gray's sweaters was even still crumpled at the foot of their bed from when they'd gotten cold in the cafeteria, and he'd given it to them. Emma had made kissy faces at Leo when she saw the exchange, and Gray had muttered, *She only sees things the way she wants to.*

He always said the right thing . . . except in that holo message. Leo picked up the sweater and held on to it. They started to get those warm feelings again. Like the next time Gray hugged them, maybe they would not let go.

Like there *had to be* another time that he hugged them.

Oof, some BESTBall would make all these nonsense feelings straighten out. Leo changed and went down to the court. They started a warm-up, back and forth from the quarter line to the center line, turning tightly with razor-sharp pivots on squeaking wheels. No one else was around, but then, everyone was moving in and hanging out with their best friends.

When someone whistled, Leo spun and caught a ball zooming at their head.

Coach Vaughn smiled. "You're on my team this season. Good to have you back where I can keep an eye on you." Only Vaughn could say this without it feeling like creepy Bixonics surveillance. The way Ace needed to trust Otis, that was the same way Leo needed to trust Vaughn.

Leo shot the ball from half-court and it nailed the scoring square. "Good to be where I'm wanted." They spoke so quietly Vaughn couldn't hear, but he could feel it. He could feel everything because of his iNsight aug.

Leo thought about asking him right then and there about the Sherlockians in his graduating class, but they thought better of it. Maybe he could tell something about that too, or at least what Leo was battling inside.

"You got your aug path settled, cadet?"

"Maybe." Leo wished the ball back into their hands, to have something to focus on beyond worries about Gray and Jayla and Ace.

Coach Vaughn snagged a ball off the rack and tossed it at them. "I'm sorry you've lost your other half."

"Not lost." Again, the words were too small for Vaughn's ears. Leo tucked the ball between their knees and shot down the court. The muscles in their arms grew warm and tight. Gray wasn't lost; he'd been taken. And there was only one way to solve it: get Sherlock . . . and break Gray free from Bixonics.

GAMBIT:
An all-out scheme

Leo rolled into the wonder of the Coliseum with the intense focus they usually saved for the court.

The place was alive with cadets trying out practice augs. One cadet shot by on TurboLegs. Someone else was swinging around a practice tail for FelineFinesse. Leo headed straight for the section beneath the blue glowing brain logo.

Something had changed since they'd come back as a third semester, an upperclassman in the program now, they were known by almost everyone. They missed the celebrity status of Gray—or maybe just the way it was hard to feel notable around him, easy to feel shielded. When a newk popped right in front of them, making their wheels squeak with a stop, they had a hard time not growling as they signed an autograph on the cadet's tablet with one finger.

They rolled into the Brain section where things were relatively calmer. Someone was trying out Mimic, playing the violin for the first time along with the holographic savant on the screen. That person had a small crowd.

Leo hoped they'd all leave them alone to try out Sherlock for the first time. Only, when they made it to the corner section under the aug's title, they found it empty apart from a table and chair. Almost like the booth had been gutted.

Leo scowled and went looking for Coach Vaughn. They found him beneath the red biceps of the Bod section, unsurprised to find Ace at the top of the flying tower, wearing the trial wings for SuperSoar, looking like he was about to toss some cookies.

Siff was at the bottom, cupping his hands to yell, "You're going to fall on your head. You need your head, Ace!"

"Stop distracting me!" Ace yelled down.

"Hey." Leo rolled to a pointed stop before their new boxmate. "Leave him alone."

Siff gestured wildly at the tower. "I'm not goading him! He's literally going to fall on his head, and spoiler alert? He needs his head."

Leo glanced up and couldn't help admitting that Siff had a point. "But you can't just stand there and holler at him. That's going to make it worse."

"I *am* actually trying to help, you know," Siff muttered

and walked away. He'd had his trial surgery for Nerve-Hack a few days prior and was sort of a new person. Leo knew that his aug had been less about becoming the superhero of his dreams like Ace and more about managing lifelong pain. He appeared to *be* a new person, but also hesitant to trust the feeling. Almost like he was worried about something else now.

Leo shook their concern away; when they had Sherlock they'd be able to help Siff and Ace. Vaughn was acting as Ace's safety tether's anchor. His thick, wide legs were planted, a line connecting him to Ace on his too-high perch. They wondered if their favorite coach was able to process more than one person's emotion at once. Right now it appeared as though he could feel every fiber of the fear that kept Ace frozen on the edge, wings poised.

"Cadet, you're going in the wrong direction." Vaughn was looking up at Ace, but Leo could tell he was talking to them.

"How so?"

"You're going to ask about Sherlock. That's the wrong direction."

"How can you tell that with your aug?"

"It's not my aug. It's experience. No one comes over here with that confused look on their face without having tried to get into the Sherlock booth. The aug is discontinued, not open to the public. Gone. A waste of a semester. Not a good choice. Too hard to get qualified for. Got it?"

Those were *a lot* of reasons, and somehow, the great big list of them added up to a dare in Leo's mind. They rolled away, uninterested in Vaughn's hesitation or whatever that was. There were lots of things about the Tower of Power that were embroiled in secrets—and almost all of them came with *Don't even think about it* warnings.

Leo returned to the empty Sherlock booth. They looked in every corner, under the chair, and finally, on the table. Two words had been scrawled in marker in a messy hand.

Try breathless breathing.

That felt like a clue. As in a scavenger hunt. Or a mystery. How very Sherlockian. Leo's brain came alive as they unpacked the possible meanings of the phrase. It made them immediately think about GillGraft, the Boost aug that let you breathe underwater.

They shot by the GillGraft booth, which had a small aquarium that cadets were dunking their heads in as they tried out the trial augs. Leo snagged one of the little devices that popped in your mouth and mimicked the experience of the aug.

They turned it over in their hand while the grad who was running the crowded booth checked their bracelets, eyeing all three. "I'd take the trial aug to the pool if I were you. These second semesters aren't getting out of the tank anytime soon."

Leo pocketed the trial aug, enjoying the freedom of

being a third semester without the pressure of making a huge, life-changing decision in fourth. They rolled down to the pool, changed into their suit, and got ready for a swim. Was this silly? What could they possibly learn about the Sherlock aug from trying out GillGraft?

Leo sat on the edge of the pool and secured their goggles first and then popped the trial aug into their mouth. The first semesters were at the far end of the pool, playing sharks and minnows with that automated, moving trapeze component that Vaughn loved.

They dove in from the edge. Beneath the blue, the water was teeming with cadets, many of whom were trying out HyperHops. That aug could launch you twenty feet with one little flick of the foot. It was pretty fun watching them zoom about, slamming into each other and spiraling beneath the surface.

Leo tried out the breathless breathing, taking water into their mouth through the aug. The device turned the water into air, and it did take a few ejected, spitted breaths before they got the hang of it. The actual aug boosted a person's lungs so that they could process the oxygen out of the water directly.

They swam down to the bottom of the pool, looking up twenty feet at the game overhead. After a few minutes, Leo started to feel foolish. How would trying out this aug help them get Sherlock?

Think, they chided themself.

Try breathless breathing.

It was a gambit, after all, and if there had been one secret message, perhaps there were more. They swam around the entire edge of the pool, searching for that scratchy handwriting. When that didn't yield anything, they went from grate to grate at the bottom.

The second to last one had a tiny bit of red on it. They swam toward it fast, already enjoying the feel of breathing underwater. This aug wasn't so fluffy. There were a lot of things that Leo could do with it, but rescue Grayson Bix didn't feel like one of them. They grabbed at the bit of red and returned to the surface with it.

With one arm braced on the pool edge, they pulled up their goggles and inspected what they'd found. It was a Bod bracelet. It had probably fallen off someone, so definitely not a clue.

Leo was just about to BESTBall toss it at the wall when they noticed a bit of scratchy handwriting inside the band.

Try all the muscles.

They crowed, rolling out of the pool and onto the deck with glee. This was . . . fun!

Within a few minutes, they were dressed and rolling back into the Coliseum. They replaced the GillGraft trial aug and went straight to the Hercules booth because that *must* be what the next clue meant. Hercules was literally *all the muscles.*

Of course, trying out Hercules was trickier than taking the Boost trial aug for a spin in the pool. To try out Hercules, Leo needed to put on this big jacket that suctioned to their arms and shoulders. It mimicked the kind of strength someone would have after their body had been amped up with mega strength and titanium-lined bones.

There was a line at this booth too, but being a third semester and BESTBall star, they cut in when someone offered. Leo put on the jacket, not really enjoying the way it pulled tight and sort of reinforced their whole body.

The grad aug at this station was busy on their tablet and did not look up. Not even when Leo jumped down from their chair, picked up the enormous mallet, and hit the strength gauge as hard as they could. The top of it lit up, blaring a carnival noise that made everyone waiting to try out the aug cheer.

Okay, that was *really* fun. No wonder so many people went for Hercules. But where would they find the next message?

Leo looked all over the weights and strength training options but found nothing. When they disengaged the trial aug jacket, peeling it off, they found one word scratched inside the tag. It was nearly worn away, nigh illegible.

Otis.

Otis? Leo left the Coliseum, this time heading straight

for Ace's BFF, otherwise known as the wild-card elevator. They were almost there when they heard Ace running up behind them.

"Wait! Leo!"

Leo slowed their roll so that Ace could catch up. He was out of breath and didn't look so great. "You okay?"

"I can't fly." His eyes got all red and his face crumpled.

Leo motioned for him to get into the elevator. Once inside they paused, and Ace sat on the floor and had a good, healthy cry.

"Maybe you're pushing yourself too hard? Gray did say that maybe humans aren't meant to fly. That aug just never . . . worked out."

"That's because it was waiting for me," Ace murmured. Leo could tell that Ace had told himself this before but that it was now becoming harder to believe. He also had something clenched in his hand.

"What's that?"

"iNsight trial aug." Ace sighed hard. "Coach Vaughn just keeps handing it to me over and over. And yeah, it helps me understand people better and interact with people better, but that's not what superheroes do. That *won't* save Gray."

Leo's chest pulled tight. "I know you want to help Gray. I get it. I do. That's all I want, but these games they make us play . . ." They stared at the elevator . . .

Otis. Ask Otis?

"Otis, how can I get the trial aug for Sherlock?"

Ace's head jerked up in surprise.

Otis said *Hmmmmmm* for so long that Leo nearly bopped an impatient fist against the wall. "I'm not so sure that's what you truly desire."

"Of course it is!" Leo surprised themself by shouting. They *never* shouted. "I've been zipping around all day, and I think you have it, so give it to me." They shot a look at Ace and then added, "Please?"

A panel popped open next to Otis's screen. Leo reached in and took out a small box. It reminded Leo of the little packages that some of the other trial augs came in. Like the one Ace was currently gripping for iNsight.

Ace got to his feet and leaned over their shoulder. "Whoa. What just happened?"

Leo held the box in front of their eyes. "The Sherlock aug has a scavenger hunt attached. I've solved it."

They opened the box, ready.

It was empty.

Ace exhaled so hard it gusted on Leo. "That's tough luck."

Leo ordered Otis back to the Coliseum level, but since they hadn't left it yet, the doors just dinged and opened. Leo shot out, heading straight for where Coach Vaughn was giving the grad augs orders for running the cleaning bots. The Coliseum was always trashed after the cadets had their way with all those delicious trial augs.

Leo shoved the empty box in his hand.

"Look at that. Record time." He didn't even seem surprised.

"Are you and Dr. Bix messing with me? If so, I'm done."

Coach Vaughn pulled up a chair and sat so that he was eye to eye with Leo. "Tell me why you want this particular aug so badly. I want to judge how honest you're willing to be."

This was a trap. He'd be able to pick up any lie, no matter how small. That was the nature of his particular aug. And Leo wasn't going to blurt out that they wanted it in order to possibly take down Bixonics, but only if the company wouldn't let Gray be free.

Leo lost the hold on their words. They were ready to give up. This was too hard. "Why'd you triple track me?"

"Why?"

"Why give me all the options if not to put it together for Sherlock?" The thought dawned on them, growing brighter and brighter. "Only a person who is triple tracked could try out all those augs and follow the scavenger hunt. *You* set me on this path. Why pull the rug out from under my wheels at the last minute?"

Coach Vaughn was ready with his answer. "Because the aug is entirely too powerful for almost everyone."

Leo wasn't prepared for that kind of honesty. It stole all their words. For a solid minute they thought about how they wanted to *know* what Rosa meant when they'd said

Everything's coming up Grayson Bix. No, not want. Need. Leo needed to know. Needed to be by his side in all this—whatever came next.

"Okay. Then tell me what happened to Felix Danvers."

Coach Vaughn was surprised, which was rare. "Felix wasn't a good fit for Sherlock. This was before we knew to rigorously screen Sherlock candidates."

"Well, what does that—"

He shook his head, cutting off Leo's daring. "Felix was a friend of mine. Tread carefully."

Leo heard that past tense. "Is he . . . gone?"

"No, but he doesn't interact with humans anymore. He lives somewhere remote, completely paid for by Dr. Bix. He was the first to try out Sherlock. He bore the brunt of the learning curve."

Leo scowled, determined even in the face of Vaughn's somberness. "But he's okay?"

"I wouldn't call a life in forced seclusion *okay.*"

"But the president. She's got Sherlock too, from *your* class. And she's okay." Well, now Leo couldn't read anything on Vaughn's face, but Leo had met Rosa. They were weird in the best way, and sure, they also lived sort of out in the middle of nowhere, but wasn't that a price Leo'd pay if it meant being able to help Grayson? To see his problems before he even had to solve them? "I know the risks, Coach. I still want to try. You know I'm no stranger to hard things."

Vaughn sighed. He even offered a small smile. What could he read in their worry, their desperation to help Gray? Not much was known about iNsight because for most people, the aug didn't do much. You had to already be empathetic for the Boost aug to create true emotional clarity.

"Please?" they added, voice small, hopes smaller.

Coach Vaughn nodded, eyes unfocused as if having a conversation with himself. "Figure out how to get Ace to fly, and you can have the trial Sherlock aug. After that, it will be up to you to get an audience with Dr. Bix. That's the only way you're getting approved for surgery, with his direct approval."

Leo's jaw nearly dropped.

Teach Ace to fly? How?

JAYLA

CRUD:
Create, Read, Update, Delete

[connectivity: Atlantis network. accessibility: extra limited.]

Jayla was *grounded*. Which was ridiculous considering she had been parenting herself since she'd joined B.E.S.T. More if you counted all those times her parents were too busy with work, which *was* important to count.

She got up and dressed just like every day since she'd moved a hundred leagues under the sea. Her mom had bought her new clothes as all the rest of her stuff had probably been confiscated by confused Bixonics employees. Then again, they must be used to tweens disappearing, leaving their possessions behind. There were hundreds of former cadets milling about this place, maybe thousands. Not that Jayla got to hang out with them. She was still on permanent watch from her suspicious parental units.

She laced up her mauve knee-high boots. Her mom

had picked them out for her, and Jayla had loved them at first sight—had actually jumped up to hug her mom in gratitude as if it were three years ago, and there wasn't so much hot water between them. That had been a good minute. There kept being these good minutes, swallowed by bad hours where her parents said no to everything she wanted to do or ask.

No, she couldn't help her dad in the lab or attend the Resistance meetings.

No, she couldn't explore Atlantis.

No, she couldn't know more about Grayson's situation.

The view out the small window in her bedroom almost felt normal now. By the calendar count, she'd been here a few weeks. Leo and Ace would be back at ToP by now after the holiday break.

How were they? Was it back to normal? Could it be?

Jayla wished she could go topside, beyond the reach of the satellite blocker, and send them a message/check for messages. But as her mom had explained, that could expose the Resistance to Bixonics. That would be bad news. For as long as Jayla could remember, the secret of her mom's movement was as important as the movement itself. If Bixonics didn't have an enemy to fight, the Resistance could keep making changes secretly. Helping people.

This had made sense when Jayla was a kid. Like a ghost attacking a giant.

But now that Jayla had seen the Bixonics side of things

at ToP, it felt more like the Resistance was a dog peeing on a building. A statement of discontent, sure. But was the Resistance stopping anything? Changing anything? Helping anyone?

Yeah, that had been last night's dinner fight.

Jayla had basically called the Resistance as corrupt as Bixonics, which she wasn't even sure she'd meant, but the damage was done. Her mom left the table without eating. Jayla sort of wished she were more like Leo and didn't say things so fast, although she knew that Leo fought their own silent battles.

The apartment was quiet, and Jayla found her dad in the kitchen, sitting at the far end of the table, scrolling through his tablet. He looked up with a grin, welcoming even after last night's debacle. "Good morning! I can't seem to get used to how good it feels to have you back."

She kissed the side of his bald head. "I know the feeling."

"Even if you're about as easy to keep an eye on as a mythological wisp."

"I'm motivated. It's a good thing." Jayla grabbed some chaos crunch cereal and poured herself a bowl. "Where's Mom?"

"Big meeting today. They're deciding . . . things I shouldn't tell you about."

"Because I can't be trusted."

"Because you don't play as a team. You're a wild card."

Her spoon paused before her mouth. "I am a team player when I get to pick my team. You and mom are still trying to make choices for me. That doesn't work. It's never worked."

Her dad nodded, taking in this information. "We don't know what to do with how grown-up you are. And you're so much like your mother when she was a kid that we're both terrified. She couldn't be stopped. Had to do everything her way."

"And now she's the Resistance leader."

"One of several important leaders. There's a committee, but I see your point."

Jayla tried to peer over his arm at his tablet, but he turned it away. "Can I go out around the deepscraper today? By myself?" She layered a smile and big eyes with those words. Her dad knew what she was up to, but that didn't mean it couldn't work.

"Oh no, today you get your wish. We're bringing you to the Resistance meeting."

Jayla was suddenly thankful that she'd picked out such a stylish outfit. "Will I get to talk with them? Find out more about Grayson?"

Dad's answer wasn't a word, but a doubtful sound.

Which proved to be true.

An hour later, Jayla was done with all adults. The committee met in her dad's lab. Jayla had sat patiently before them while they discussed the unique situation of her aug, and how it appeared as though she was not being tracked like everyone else.

"But we know that there are improvements being made to the aug tracking software," a tall, masculine person pointed out. "Perhaps the tracking software is harder to detect."

"We could take her out beyond the satellite blocker and see if the reclamation personnel show up," someone else threw in.

"Use my daughter as bait?" Jayla's mom clarified with a crisp tone. "Is that what you're suggesting?"

Jayla smooshed her lips together to keep from yelling that her aug was no sleeper agent. She'd literally deleted all the Bixonics software. There was nothing left to be sneaky. At least Amir understood.

Their gazes met for a minute. He raised his hand. Amir was only fifteen, but the Resistance members listened to him. Probably because he had become their prized ToP double agent more than a year ago. The role Jayla had always imagined for herself.

Her mom called on Amir. "I believe that Jayla is not sending out any location signals whatsoever. I've triple-checked. I have scans to offer if anyone would like to see them."

The tall person sat even taller, their head higher than everyone else's. "And yet you were the one who pointed out that they're coming up with new ways to track cadets.

By your own logic, you could be wrong."

Amir sighed and shrugged. They'd been dancing around this forever.

When the meeting took a break, Jayla made an escape. She wasn't surprised to find Amir tailing her, and she even slowed down to let him catch up. "Can you take me to the cadet level?"

"Your parents still haven't given you a hall pass?"

"I'm not trustworthy or whatever." She shook her head, and they crossed to the elevator. Once they reached sublevel seventy-four, Jayla leaned on the balcony overlooking the former cadets as they played SAR and competed with their augs and laughed. Most of them looked okay with being locked down here, but how could it be okay for the rest of their lives? "What did they mean by *reclamation personnel*?"

"They're like a Bixonics SWAT team. Whenever they pick up a signal of a rogue aug, they fly in and make that person disappear. Sometimes they're never seen again. Other times, they get rereleased into the world with a *very* different attitude about the corporation."

So this was why everyone was so scared? There were hundreds of augged people here who were not functioning as a part of the Bixonics empire. They deserved freedom too. "We need to find a way to free them."

Amir didn't respond. Probably because they still needed to find a way to free *him*. Deleting the tracking software on Amir's XConnect wasn't as easy as it had been on Jayla's. Especially because she couldn't check the stream of numbers and commands on his interface anymore. It was all in his head.

"Any progress on your network?" she asked.

He nodded. As a last-ditch attempt to free his aug, Jayla was having him create his own independent network like Jayla had done before leaving ToP. "It's coming along. I'll show you."

They went down to the main floor, moving around former cadets, and entered the holo-room. Amir washed the little cubicle a sandy, burned-orange, which reminded Jayla of camel fur.

"'This is the exact holo-room they have at ToP," she wondered aloud without processing the words. She remembered coloring the whole place blueberry over and over as she created her own system without alerting the Bixonics software inside her own body. It had been like cutting out a cancer: messy, hard, but important work.

"Suppose they have the same supplier." Amir shrugged. He showed her what he'd been working on since the other day when they'd checked in with each other. Jayla had to admit that she liked spending time with Amir. He was two years older and being with him made her feel older . . . whereas her parents had the uncanny ability to make her feel like she was still five. "Any luck on your work?" Amir asked.

Jayla glanced at the interface on her arm. "I don't think

I'll be able to get anywhere until they let my aug sync up with the network down here."

That was half true. She didn't want to admit that she was having zero luck writing code in her head. It was total CRUD all day long. She'd tried all of Amir's visual techniques. Apparently he could see a chalkboard in his head, writing code along it mentally, erasing pieces when they needed to be changed.

Jayla's brain didn't seem to work that way. She shook off her worries and looked around at the construction of Amir's new network. He was able to throw all the code up around them in the holo-room so that she could double-check it. "This is solid," she diagnosed after a minute. "It's still rudimentary, and you'll have to reinvent a whole lot of programs, but I think you're ready to delete the Bixonics software."

She turned to face Amir; he looked scared.

"I've seen augs get corrupted when we delete the tracking software," he said. "The people . . . well, it's painful and sometimes ends badly."

Jayla didn't know what *that* meant, but she'd seen augs gone wrong before. For example, there was a young former cadet currently running spastic circles outside the holo-room on TurboLegs that were most certainly misfiring. "Look, I know it's scary, but this is how I did it. I created my own stuff and deleted *all* their stuff."

Amir exhaled hard. He sat cross-legged in the center of

the room and closed his eyes. She knew what that meant.

"Are you doing it now?"

He nodded.

Jayla had the funniest urge to give him a good-luck hug. She sat cross-legged in front of him, knees to knees. "I'm here if you need me."

One little corner of his mouth lifted in a smile, and Jayla grinned back.

Minutes later, Amir opened his eyes. His gaze looked different, more direct, but everything else felt the same. "Did it work?" she asked.

"Everything's running slower. I've got a lot of code checking to do, but if it works, we should call a Resistance meeting to show them."

"Not until we're sure it worked," she said. "They're too excited to shoot things down."

Amir looked thoughtful. "I know how to make sure. And you can check on your friends while we're at it."

The tendersub surfaced, the water parting like crystal curtains. Jayla enjoyed how different it felt now, when compared with last time.

There had been so much rush to get Leo and Ace back to ToP. So much fear about Grayson's situation. Now she felt . . . between worlds. Between Bixonics and the Resistance. Did she have to pick a side like everyone else?

The tendersub bobbed along on the surface. They were

miles from her dad's prized satellite blocker and the little island that sort of camouflaged the top of the deepscraper. For all her excitement about linking up to the world again, she was a little afraid to log back in to humanity.

"If we catch any incoming air traffic, we dive," Amir said. "I think we can disappear in a hurry, but it's still risky." He checked the sky over and over. But no one came. Maybe he *was* free.

Maybe they'd done it!

Jayla surprised herself by wanting to run straight to her parents and tell them, but the last few weeks had created a strange standoff. She wanted to help, and she felt certain that any technology she'd created to do so might be taken away and used without her. She wasn't going to be left out of this ever again.

"What if it worked?" Amir asked, staring at the empty, blue sky, contemplating his own freedom.

Jayla's plan was ready. "Then we help the others. We don't go to the Resistance if they're going to be so hard to work with. We help the other XConnects create their own software and delete the old stuff, then they help us write new code for all the augs."

Amir blinked, such rich green eyes by the light of the actual sun. Oh, Jayla had missed the *real* sun. There were vitamin D lamps all over the place in Atlantis, but it was nothing compared to the real thing.

The warmth and golden light filled Jayla with bravery. She opened her network back up.

[connectivity: world wide web. accessibility: unlimited.]

Jayla jumped when her network started flooding her senses with articles, ads, newsletters, and messages. She went for the most important first.

[inbox: one hundred seventy-two unviewed direct messages]

"One hundred and seventy-two!" Jayla flicked through the list. Most of them were from Ace, ideas he had that were then counterpointed by his next ideas. She got to one with the subject line EMERGENCY and clicked play. The image appeared on her interface, even though she knew she could close her eyes and watch it in her mind. Ace was pacing about his room, hands gesturing everywhere.

"Jayla, we're back at school and GUESS WHO our new boxmates are!" Ace filled Jayla in on Siff and Emma. He seemed to think that these two had been reassigned to spy on Lilliput, but Leo disagreed. Where was Leo? Surely they should be keeping an eye on Ace and at the very least stopping him from sending seventy-one nonessential messages to her top-secret network in less than three weeks.

Ace finished by slumping onto his bed, jaw propped on his fists. "I'm worried about Leo. They're obsessed with getting Sherlock. Like *obsessed*. But we're going down to the Coliseum in a few. Maybe I can get them to try a different aug." He sounded so doubtful. Ace was *never* doubtful.

That message was from five days ago.

When Jayla looked up, she was shocked to find that she was no longer in her box with a wild-eyed Ace but bobbing on the ocean with Amir.

Jayla flicked through the messages again, hoping for a missed one from Grayson.

There was nothing from Leo either, which didn't feel right, but then maybe they'd been listening when she told the boxmates that this network was for emergencies only.

Oh, Ace. She had to agree with him. There's no way his archnemesis and Leo's evil twin were in their box by accident. Maybe Leo hadn't said anything because they thought they *could* handle it. Maybe they could handle it; they were Leo after all. But then, what about Ace? It wasn't a good sign that he was nervous.

Jayla covered her face with her hands.

"Bad news?" Amir asked.

"Maybe. Maybe not." Jayla thought for a minute. She'd been so desperate to reconnect with the world that this felt oddly . . . a little wrong. Her heart hammered suddenly. She *did not* want to get caught out here, disobeying her parents after they'd begun to trust her enough to bring her into an actual meeting. "We should go."

The tendersub headed straight back to Atlantis on

autopilot, drawing them deeper and deeper. Jayla had to admit that spending a few weeks with her parents had made her a lot less daring. She'd needed to connect to the outside world for a spell, but she didn't want to hurt her parents again. *Ever* again. Her heart continued to hammer as the view through the window grew as dark as endless black.

Jayla sketched out a brand-new code: how to join Team Resistance—and therefore her parents.

11

FUNCTION:
Code with a role

Amir and Jayla were inseparable for the next few weeks. They created a two-person anti-Bixonics campaign, recruiting fellow XConnects from the cadet level.

It took the Resistance a long time to catch on to what they were doing, and by that point, Jayla was more than ready. Amir joked that they'd made themselves a little army, but it did feel like she had backup forces when she marched into the latest, stiff committee meeting with thirteen cadets who were no longer transmitting their location—apart from the one they were about to free.

No matter what the Resistance scientists tried, they could not find any sign of the software that should've pinpointed where they were.

Jayla's mom's jaw was one of the first to drop to the floor. "And you can do this for the others?" she asked. "How?"

Jayla glanced at Amir, who nodded encouragingly. "The way our aug works, we simply needed to make new operating software and delete the old stuff. That's easy for us because . . . well, our aug makes it easy."

"How could you possibly do that for others?" that tall doubty-butt person threw in, but Jayla was ready.

"Thomie?" she called out. One of the youngest augged cadets came forward. He was twelve. He'd had his surgery early during second semester, with special permission, but that had gotten him in over his head. His TurboLegs were strong and fast, and he couldn't seem to get any control over them, randomly running in circles at top speed.

Thomie sat before the audience of Resistance scowls with big eyes. Jayla flipped on the machine that picked up tracking signals coming out of the cadet, and it beeped a slow, steady warning.

"So, I'm going to link up with the software that runs the hardware in Thomie's legs. Amir and I have written new code for him, especially since the old stuff is so amped up that it keeps malfunctioning." Jayla worked her magic. This was the first cadet they'd tried to help who didn't have an XConnect aug, but she was certain if she took the time to adjust the function on some of these augs, they'd not only be free of the tracking software, they'd also be more manageable in general.

After a few minutes, the beeping that indicated Thomie's active tracking software dulled and disappeared.

She pushed past the moment where it felt like Thomie was a puppet who'd had their strings cut—when the aug had no software to run—and then uploaded her own code.

After a minute, the kid lifted his head and grinned. "I feel better!"

"Try running," Amir said.

Thomie looked like he was scared to, and who blamed him after he'd run into so many walls? After a second, he zipped around the meeting room. And then the door blew open and he was gone.

Jayla laughed. "There's one more done. What say you all help us do this and stop making us work in secret?" She didn't mean to stare straight at her mom when she said this, and yet that's exactly what happened.

Her mom kept her chin firmly raised, her eyes hard and daring. And then she said, "I call the vote. Who is in favor of allowing my daughter to delete the tracking software on the cadets in our care?"

Hands went up. Many hands. They wanted her to do it!

The meeting adjourned soon thereafter. Jayla bumped fists with Amir, and her dad brought her a lab coat, symbolically and literally welcoming her to the science team of Atlantis. All that was great, but none of it was greater than the way her mom had said *my daughter*, so full of pride. It might easily be the best present she'd ever received.

Better than her new lucky boots.

Weeks later, Jayla and Amir's technique had spread throughout the lab, and her army of XConnects, with the help of the Resistance scientists under Jayla's dad, had freed most of the former cadets in New Atlantis.

This success seemed to lighten everything in the deep-scraper. There was hope now. Real, tangible hope for a world with augs that weren't controlled by Bixonics.

And Jayla was the reason for that hope.

But she was also exhausted. She nearly passed on the opportunity to do one more reprogramming that evening, but her dad had said this would be a special one.

The former cadet was older, maybe early twenties, and was introduced to her as one of the guardians of Atlantis. The guards who lived topside and managed things.

"Rosa has a special aug. One you haven't written code for yet." Her dad spoke as if he were still a doctor at heart even though he'd spent the last few years in the lab. "You feeling up to this, Rosa?"

"Yeah, sure. My brain hurts, but you already know that." Rosa narrowed her eyes at Jayla. "What's your daughter doing here?"

"How'd you know I'm his daughter?" Jayla asked.

"Because I've got eyes."

"Eyes and Sherlock," her dad added. "Rosa is one step ahead of us all the time. Which makes them grouchy and misunderstood *all* the time." Her dad delivered this information partly in awe and partly in warning.

"Nah, I'm one step ahead of Bixonics all the time. You know why."

"Sherlock?" Jayla asked, stunned.

Amir popped his head over the top of the workstation. "Did you say there is someone here with Sherlock?"

Rosa growled and threw her arms over her head. "Stop. Overwhelmed. Stop."

Jayla's dad ushered Jayla out of the workstation, motioning for Amir to join them as well. "Rosa's circuits get fried easily. She can't stop taking in and sorting information, so being around other people is *very* hard."

"That's why she works topside?" Amir asked like he already knew the answer.

Jayla's dad nodded. "See what you can do with their aug, but go easy on yourselves. I won't be surprised if this is one you can't fix."

Well, now that was just a dare.

But it was a good one because days later, Jayla was still struggling to find the parameters of the Sherlock software. "It takes up five hundred times the memory of the other augs." She tried to explain to her dad. "Amir and I can barely put all the code together, let alone isolate it."

All the while that they worked, Rosa slept like she were dead.

"She's so tired," Amir noted.

"Her aug runs all the time. Constantly draining." Jayla's dad was trying something on his tablet; he'd been trying to be helpful and in the process had sort of become his daughter's assistant. She loved it. "Your aug works the same, doesn't it? But you're younger so it's easier to bear. Lance was so dazzled by the ability to augment humans that he never stopped to wonder what it would cost. Rosa's body is very busy running this Brain aug. Too busy to run her body sometimes. And then there's the constant over-whelming by too much information."

Jayla had forgotten that sometimes her dad called Dr. Bix "Lance"; she had forgotten that when they were younger, they knew each other. Well, now Dr. Bix was an established millionaire scientist who'd invented Bixonium. And her dad was a progressive doctor who'd started off in the med center at ToP—and then got rescued by her mom. She felt warm; that was still such a romantic story. Jayla wanted to hear her mom tell it again, like she used to when Jayla was small and in love with their love.

For some reason she looked at Amir, and he looked at her, and Jayla's nerves danced. She pressed herself into her work, but no matter what she tried or how many XCon-nects she linked together, the aug was too powerful to alter.

"I should've known." Jayla's mom came to see how it was going one slow afternoon. "We had to fake Rosa's death you know. She's one of the only Sherlocks out there, and I think they would have tracked her to outer space."

Jayla was a little shocked.

And then her stomach dropped out the bottom of her

body. She'd been so tired, so overworked that she'd forgotten something super crucial.

"Leo is trying for Sherlock."

"Leo your boxmate?"

"They won't succeed," her dad added quickly. "That aug has been discontinued." He motioned to Rosa, who was sleeping with their mouth open. "For obvious reasons."

Jayla thought about the president, who famously had Sherlock. How was she so functional and Rosa . . . wasn't? What would happen to Leo if they *did* succeed?

Leo was impossible to stop when they set their mind on something.

"They will," Rosa said sleepily. "Succeed. I could tell the first time I met them."

Now Jayla had shivers, thinking about Ace's worried messages. She really needed to pop topside and check on things at ToP—and warn Leo off trying to get this darn aug. There would be time, though. Any aug Leo picked wouldn't be permanent and irreversible until next semester.

Before she could think on that more, Jayla had to admit to her parents that she couldn't free Rosa from the tracker. It was a miserable admission, and tears just fell out of her eyes. Her parents looped their arms around her, cushioning her failure with their love.

She cried hard from a powerful accumulation of exhaustion and disappointment. "I'm so worried about Ace and Leo at ToP. Not to mention Gray, who is still out there somewhere." How could she help him if she still didn't know where he was or what he was doing?

Her mom kissed her cheeks. "Well, I think we can help you feel better. And I think you've more than earned our trust in this."

Jayla was too tired to unpack that. Too tired to notice when they took the elevator, not to their little apartment that was slowly starting to feel like home, but to an empty sublevel that had guards outside the door.

She barely registered when her parents talked. "Amir just unlocked his tracking software. There was an additional feed on his aug that meant we needed to keep him away from everything else. A constantly streaming surveillance video that fed straight to Bixonics headquarters. We didn't know how deep it went, but your technique has set him free. We're pretty confident of that."

"Who?" Jayla asked blearily. Her parents were being extra cagey. "Who are you talking about?"

Her dad opened the seven locks on the door, and then he stood back. Jayla's mom put a gentle hand on her back. Jayla took a step inside.

And there was Grayson Bix, sitting on a couch, playing video games.

12

CONDITIONALS:
Who's in control here?

Grayson and Jayla ran at each other. They hugged and hugged. Then Jayla spun around to give her parents a piece of her mind. How could they have hidden the fact that Grayson was here—had been this whole time!

Gray grabbed her hand, making her pause. "My VisionX was like a video camera, Jayla. They had to figure out how to stop it before I could be around anyone else. Even with the satellite blocker and the ocean, the signal was *so strong.*"

That was a good excuse, and yet it was also an excuse, so Jayla hated it.

"They could have told me." Her parents had conveniently stayed in the hall. Gray and Jayla sat on a couch, catching each other up on everything. By the time Jayla had finished the tale of the failed rescue mission and Ace's shoestring, they were both laughing again like they were back in Lilliput.

"Is Leo okay?" Gray asked, wiping laughter-tears from his eyes.

Jayla thought for a minute. "I don't know, but I think we need to send a message to ToP as soon as possible. I'm worried for them."

"That's not the only worrying thing." Grayson stared at his hands. "My mom . . . well, she was sick, and a few days ago, she sort of fell asleep and wouldn't wake up. They took her away, and I don't know what's going on. I'm scared to ask."

Jayla wasn't ready for that to be the end of the story. She pulled the security door open and found her parents still standing there, as if they'd been prepared for this question too. "Where's Gray's mom?"

"Come with us." Jayla's mom held out a hand, and Jayla took it, worried that things were about to get really dark.

The four of them took the elevator up the deepscraper to a different level than the med center. Jayla didn't have a great feeling about that . . . certainly Gray's mom should be there, right?

The elevator wouldn't unlock without a different code from both of Jayla's parents. She expected the doors to open to a top-security center, but the level was empty apart from a series of large metal pillars.

When Jayla walked too close to one, it emanated frigid air. "What is this place?"

Jayla's parents surrounded Gray and Jayla. Every single thing they did was cautious and sent alarm bells through her body and therefore her network.

"Grayson," Jayla's mom took his hands in hers. "This is going to be very hard, but I want you to understand that your mom is not gone. Not dead. Merrida is being preserved until we know how to cure her Bixonium poisoning."

"Preserved?! Bixonium poisoning!" Jayla shouted, making everyone jump.

Jayla's dad clasped a hand on her shoulder to comfort her, and maybe to let her know that she'd get more info about everything later.

Grayson nodded. Jayla's dad touched a small button, opening a view of one of the metal pillars. Inside was Grayson's mom, frozen peacefully in cryo sleep.

Jayla's mouth fell open.

Grayson touched the glass. He didn't cry, but maybe that's because his mom's state was so hard to process. She wasn't dead . . . but she wasn't alive right now either, was she?

"We're going to find a way to save her," Jayla whispered.

Grayson stared and stared. "My dad did this to her."

Jayla's dad came forward to comfort Grayson. "Lance didn't know that Bixonium would sneak into him a little at a time. He didn't know that he'd take it home to her. That's the problem with brand-new science. There are brand-new problems."

Grayson looked confused. "But if she got sick, why didn't he? Let me guess: he had some wild cure, but he kept it for himself?"

Jayla's mom and dad exchanged long looks.

"What?" Jayla nearly yelled.

Her dad touched a button on another pillar, and this time, Jayla and Grayson were looking straight at a frozen Dr. Lance Bix.

"Dad!" Gray cried out, rushing toward the pillar. "When did this happen? Why is he here? Are you holding him hostage?"

"It's best if he explains it to you himself." Jayla's mom used a control panel on the pillar to pull up a holographic message.

A life-size Dr. Bix appeared in front of them, smiling—and looking very ill. The technology was so good that he looked *real*. Of course, Jayla had seen his holographic image at ToP events, but she'd assumed it was because he was too busy to visit the program, not because he *couldn't*.

"Hello, Grayson, my son. I am so sorry for this shock. I've recorded this message to hopefully explain how we've come to this reality . . . The truth is that Bixonium is far more dangerous than I ever knew it could be. Well, obviously I did not do well with this gamble. The corporation does not want anyone to learn about the poisoning. It would ruin the story of this strange little empire. The chips would fall fast. They would see that mining for Bixonium caused tsunamis. Eruptions. They'd find all the cadets whose augs didn't quite take or had learned too much and escaped. If the company feels threatened, they'll call up their army. Control every single augged person on the planet with the flick of a switch." Dr. Bix's voice never faltered in all that, but the hologram of him sat down abruptly after a seat appeared beneath the good scientist.

Jayla's dad paused the video. Everyone gave Grayson a minute to process.

"I'm okay. Put it back on." He kept his head low, cracked his knuckles.

Jayla's mom nodded and motioned for Jayla's dad to restart the video.

Dr. Bix's hologram smiled wearily until Jayla's dad pressed play. "The corporation does not know that I created the Resistance and funded the renovation of Atlantis to hopefully gain back some control over the company. Once the company went public, the profits became more important than the science. Augs are not dangerous . . . unless they're being pushed forward in the wrong hands. Controlled by the wrong people. The technology is barreling ahead of the scientific understanding, and I'm grateful for my friends who have helped keep these secrets—and created new hope for our future."

Jayla looked at her parents. They were his *friends*? All this time?

"I'm sorry for all these secrets, son. I am so sorry about your mother."

Now Grayson was crying, and Jayla put her arms around him tightly.

"The people here are working hard to find a way to undermine the power of the corporation, to help cadets who get in over their head, and perhaps not the most pressing issue, but one I'm personally invested in"—he chuckled sadly—"they are also trying to find a way to save us."

Jayla's mind wandered as the rest of the message turned personal and only for Grayson, which worked out well because her thoughts were on fire.

Her mom's voice was calming and a little . . . guilty sounding? "We're sorry we had to keep this all from you both. It's a lot, we know."

For once, Jayla understood her parents' secrecy. The Resistance *was* Bixonics . . . or maybe its secret better half? She couldn't even find the words to form the questions. Everything Jayla knew had changed . . . but had she been expecting something like this all along? Was this the reason she had never been able to *choose sides* like all those around her seemed to have done?

"Strangely enough, I'm not that surprised. Okay, popsicle humans were a bit of a surprise." She stepped back farther from Gray to whisper, "How long has Dr. Bix been frozen?"

"A few months," her dad said softly. "His poisoning was worse than Grayson's mom's."

Jayla's mind whirled. "But we've seen Dr. Bix since then! His hologram is always popping up around ToP, giving speeches!"

"The Dr. Bix hologram is a puppet software that they use at B.E.S.T. and other strongholds of the corporation." Her mother's frown was deep. "Dr. Bix developed it himself, but it's being used differently now."

Jayla gasped. "The company is using it like a puppet?"

"The company is, yes, but that's not the part that's truly troubling."

"It's the puppeteer." Gray reentered their company, clenching his hands.

Jayla's dad nodded. "Yes, the puppeteer. We have a few guesses who it could be. The person at the very top must be special. Or especially powerful. The secrecy *inside* the corporation is alarming alone. Then again, we're pretty sure no one knows about Atlantis or the cryostasis chambers, so that's in our favor."

Gray nodded, seeming to decide something. "I'm going to find this person who's using my dad's image. Before they have a reason to raise that terrifying global army my dad accidentally Frankensteined into existence."

Jayla barked a surprised—and delighted—laugh.

Grayson's smile was firm. "Guess I should figure out how to take over my dad's company like I was raised to do. I'll need Leo. I think best with Leo." He glanced back at the twin tanks containing his frozen parents. "Jayla? You have to find a way to save them, please?"

—LEVEL THREE:

SUNLIGHT ZONE

LEO

13

EYE ON THE BALL:
Full focus, making a difference

Leo was trying reverse psychology. "Ace, no one has ever mastered those wings in the eleven years it's been available. It might not be possible. You should give up."

The Coliseum was cavernous when empty. Everyone was watching or participating in the aug–water polo tournament down at the pool level. Well, everyone but them two, it seemed.

"I should give up?" Leo could hear how Ace's voice shook even from three stories in the air.

"Ah, no," Leo called up quickly. "That was not cool. Just trying to . . ."

Ace sat on the edge of the platform at the top of the SuperSoar tower, frown puckered, wings folded at his side like the saddest little gargoyle. "You were trying to trick me. Finn does that reverse thinking on me all the time." He sounded so tired. They had been at it for an hour, and this was their fifth time trying that week, but at least his arms *were* a lot stronger now. "Mama Jay says it's mean to do that. You're pushing with your feelings."

Leo reddened; he was right. They shouldn't be working him so hard . . . or they should *tell him* about their deal with Vaughn to get that trial aug. That would at least give Ace context about their urgency. "Sorry. I just thought it might motivate you to hear that it's impossible."

"Why would that motivate me?" Ace squeaked.

Leo shrugged. Stuff like that always motivated them. They should have felt bad about spending every free moment helping Ace learn to fly. It'd already taken them away from the BESTBall season a little too much, but their team was doing well. They might even make it into the championship in a few weeks.

Ace had conquered his fear of heights, though, so that was a win. He kicked his dangling legs. "I know what's going to happen. I'm not going to get my wings. I'm going to get stuck with iNsight because it's the only thing I'm good at. Having feelings. Helping people with *feelings*."

He said the word *feelings* like it was *anchovies*.

"Yeah, but look how much good Vaughn has done with iNsight."

"Yeah. Guess so."

They were losing him. *Eye on the ball, Leo!*

They tried to think like they already had Sherlock. It was a game that had gotten a little addictive lately. Ace *was* a natural at iNsight. Whenever he turned the trial bud back in, Vaughn gave it back. Even Leo had to admit that Ace seemed to have laser-like perception about the people around him when he was wearing it. It'd even helped him become friends with Siff!

"Ace. Maybe you just need a pep talk. Think about the impossible things you have done. You regularly hang out with Siff now. You've made friends with your archnemesis!"

"He's only pretending to be my friend. He stole all my best SAR cards yesterday when he thought I was getting a snack. He felt bad about it, but he didn't give them back and kept trying to lie about having them. When a person lies, their aura gets all puke green."

iNsight helped you understand when a person was lying. That would be interesting information to have, but it still wasn't better than the siren song of the Sherlock aug. "Their aura?"

"Yeah, the more I use the trial bud, the more I see emotions in light spectrums." Only Ace could say this glumly, chin propped on his knuckles, lips puckered in a pout. "Vaughn says it's different for him. He thinks I might have synesthesia. Where your senses do different things than other people's. They can add it to my list of neurodivergences. It's getting to be a long list!"

Leo knew what synesthesia was, but they let him explain. A new plan was forming in their mind. Ace got overwhelmed by his feelings so often. Was that happening every time he looked over the edge? "Ace, what do you feel when you step off the platform and try to flap those wings?"

"Fear, excitement, more fear. A whole mess of nerves, honestly."

"What color is it?"

Ace scowled down at them. "What color is my fear?"

"Yeah."

Leo watched as Ace begrudgingly took the trial bud out of his pocket. He popped it into his ear and zoned out for a minute while the tech acclimated to his body. Then he stood, toes over the edge, held out his parachute-lined arms, and looked down.

First, he took in the empty Coliseum. Next, he looked at his own chest. "Blue. I'm all blue."

"Blue like the sky?" Leo called up.

Ace's mouth twitched with a smile. "Blue like the sky," he repeated sweetly, almost too quiet for Leo to hear. They weren't even ready when Ace dove off the platform. His technique was excellent—they'd done so much work on being streamlined and then lifted like a leaf on the wind.

For the first time since Leo had started watching him dive from that great height with nothing but a tether keeping him back from a terrible fall, they were more excited than afraid for him. This part they'd achieved before—the dive and then the glide.

The flapping is where it all usually went wrong.

Ace did a full gliding circle, the tether controlling how far he could go . . . and then he gave a little flap. A tiny one! How long had Leo tried to convince him to do *a small* move? Dear, old Ace always went for the gusto!

He flapped once and lifted higher in his circle, then returned to a gliding circle.

"Leo!" Ace screeched happily.

"Try again! Just a little more this time!" they called up.

Ace waited for the right moment like they'd practiced. He felt for it; Leo could tell even from the floor of the Coliseum that it might actually work. They held their breath.

Ace flapped—harder than he should—shooting up toward the ceiling. He nearly collided with the domed roof of the Coliseum, only to turn by himself, dropping toward the ground fast.

Then his wings filled *out* and his small body hung above Leo's head like a . . . bird.

He circled lower and lower, and Leo let out the line that allowed Ace to reach the floor. By the time he landed on his actual feet, they were both screaming.

Leo grabbed his shoulders and shook him happily. Ace threw out his winged arms and crowed. They couldn't help wishing that Gray and Jayla were here to see this. Ace started to cry with joy and hugged on Leo.

"You turn purple when you're happy!" he said right in their ear.

"Purple, huh?" A voice spoke behind him.

Leo and Ace packed in their celebration and turned to face their silent spectator. Leo wasn't surprised to find Vaughn giving them a slow, affirming clap.

Ace ran to the coach, then hugged him around the stomach, making the older man say *oof* and then pat Ace's back encouragingly.

"Out of that gear, cadet." Vaughn was trying to put some gruff on top of his sweet, and it made him sound even sweeter. "Better go spread the word that we've got our first successful series of flaps on SuperSoar."

Ace was already shedding gear, peeling straight for the exit.

"Otis is going to be so happy for me!" he yelled, already out the door.

Leo giggled. That AI really was his best friend here.

Vaughn had recovered from Ace bouncing off his hard, round stomach and was eyeing Leo with resignation and a deep sigh. "How'd you crack it?"

"His feelings were tripping him up. Overwhelming him. He used the iNsight trial aug to figure out how to trust himself." Leo looked up with all their expressions tucked neatly inside. They wanted one feeling to permeate Vaughn's heightened senses: success.

"Roll with me, Leo." Coach Vaughn rarely spoke their first name. It had a strangely calming effect. They left the Coliseum together—instead of going to the empty Sherlock booth, they noted—and turned down the hall to the elevator that was specifically for administration.

Leo hadn't been in it before. Unlike Otis, it had old-school buttons instead of an erratic robotic voice. They got off on floor thirty-seven. Leo had never been here before either. The whole level seemed deserted. No cadets. No grad augs running about, keeping order. No teachers or coaches.

"With Sherlock you'll always know too much," Coach Vaughn started.

Leo let his words sink a little before saying, "Like how you know too much because of your aug. And you're okay."

"The only person happy knowing too much is the person who is happy knowing too little. Does that describe you, Leo?"

"But we don't pick augs to make us happy. Otherwise you would have given Ace a pass for SuperSoar a semester ago."

"You're asking for danger. There's no way around it. It's dangerous. It makes people dangerous. Felix became dangerous overnight. If Ace gets approved for those wings—and god help us if he does—he'll crash many times. Break bones and bash his head. That's a terrifying thought because I care about that little hero, but it's nothing compared to the fear that I have giving you this."

Coach Vaughn held out a little tiny earbud. It looked like the iNsight trial aug.

"Your brain is about to become a supercomputer, cadet.

I hope this is what you actually wanted."

A shiver spread down Leo's arms. The piece of tech was so small and cold and heavy. Leo looked up into their coach's nervous eyes. "I'll be careful."

"There's more." The way he said it seemed to mean that everything before had been the buildup. Time for whatever blow he was holding back.

"What is it?"

Vaughn moved to a locked door and entered a bunch of codes, then even did an eyeball scan to get the door to open. What could possibly be behind it?

When the door opened and Leo rolled in, they were shocked to find nothing but a display panel and a few rows of plush theater-style chairs. They rolled up to the open spot for wheelchairs and put the break on. They didn't use the break much; Vaughn knew this. He watched them do it as if Leo were further cementing their decision.

"Put it in your ear when the video tells you to." He looked a million years old all of a sudden. "Watch until the end. Your training will bring you here every single day for six hours a day. There won't be anyone else around, and that is on purpose. You're not ready to let the aug loose on others. You won't be ready for that for weeks, possibly not until you have the surgery. We'll see." He put a hand over his face. What feelings was he picking up from Leo? Fear, excitement, victory? All three?

He left, the door slammed, and the room became very

dark. The bud was so small and innocent seeming. They turned it over in their hands, finding the tiny letters on one side that labeled it as Sherlock. For all the warnings, Leo still wanted it. Still badly wanted to be the number-one person who could help Grayson Bix. No, they needed it.

The wall-size holoscreen turned on after a minute. Words flowed across the screen: *Place your Sherlock trial aug firmly in your ear.*

And Leo did.

14

PUNCH-DRUNK:
Lost in the heat of the game

They were down by two points; Leo didn't know what was going on with their teammates. The first half of the championship game wrapped, signaled by a tone that blared through the BESTBall stadium.

While the stands emptied toward bathrooms and concessions, Leo rolled into the locker room at the back of the pack of their weary teammates. Once inside, they drank water, alone in the corner where they preferred to regroup. The rest of the team knew that even though they were the captain, they weren't about to give any speeches or pep talks or advice. That would mean talking.

And for all the wondrous things that the Sherlock trial bud had brought to Leo's life, being able to express how they were feeling or what they were thinking was not one of them. But that was the thing about Sherlock. When they had the bud in, they didn't have to find ways to communicate because they already knew what was going on. They could skip straight to *making a move*.

It's like this aug was made for Leo!

They eyed the little silver bud sitting on the shelf in their locker. They'd promised Vaughn that they wouldn't use it outside of the weird, boring training room where they solved maze-like simulations and saved the Bixonics-green puppy.

Leo had no idea how six hours passed every time they were in there. It was sort of interesting, sort of super boring. Mostly it taught information about the creation of Bixonics. Why did someone who wanted a Sherlock aug need to learn way too much about the inner workings of the company? Great question. And the trial bud had already sorted out the answer. Because when they got Sherlock, they would be an important asset to the company. Naturally. Think of all the good they could do for Bixonics.

By saving the green puppy.

They knew that sounded weird. They didn't bother telling anyone else about the long company history and values sessions, with only the briefest breaks to save a puppy. There was always this puppy about to fall into a hole or jump off a roof. Leo learned fast that the name of the game was to save the puppy. Even when the room was full of very realistic puppies in very realistic fire peril, Leo knew that it would be over swiftly when they reached down and saved the green one.

But *only* the green one.

Last night they'd dreamed about ruling Bixonics with Grayson on their left and their Bixonics-green hound on their right. They'd woken up with their heart pounding, their championship nerves completely rerouted from the, you know, small fact that their team was in the championships.

Now Leo couldn't wait for this game to be over so they could get back to training. They frowned into the smelly depths of their locker. How could they love their aug more than BESTBall already? Weird.

Vaughn was giving the team a gravelly pep talk, and they itched to grab the trial bud and give it just three minutes in their ear. Then they'd know *exactly* why their teammates were acting sluggish and uncooperative, and they could solve the problems, get the win.

"Captain." Vaughn's voice was punchy. "Care to leave your locker to its secrets and join the team?"

Leo didn't mean to glare at Vaughn. It just happened. They had the shortest temper right now. Sherlock had told them it was because they were growing and changing fast. It was all normal, part and parcel with becoming invincible.

Vaughn's eyebrow raised in response, but Leo was saved from the trouble as the youngest member of the team pulled off the bandage on her elbow with her teeth, revealing fresh blood on an old game injury.

Vaughn started patching her up, and Leo pretended to grab some more water. They pocketed the trial bud. They weren't going to use it on the court, of course. But what was the harm in keeping it in their pocket when they played?

They'd only been using the Sherlock trial bud for three weeks, but they already felt incomplete without it. When it was inside them, they wouldn't have to worry. They couldn't wait until surgery. Leo was about to become the sharpest tool in Bixonics's empire. They wouldn't have to go home anymore if they didn't want to. They'd find Gray in a blink . . . and they'd be able to stop Emma from getting to them ever again.

Leo and their team wheeled out of the locker room to catch the very end of the halftime show. The cheer squad was finishing up a dramatic number. Several of them were showing off their trial augs, which helped them make twenty-foot-high throws and catches.

The cheer captain was another nonbinary cadet like Leo. They had the FelineFinesse aug and were proving just how high they could drop from and still land on their feet. Their biologically grafted tech tail swished in a grand finale. The music hit a lighting cue at the exact right moment, and the crowd erupted. A two-second blackout let the squad scurry off the court.

"Leo." Coach Vaughn hustled over as the lights turned back on, and many cadets shot toward the stadium doors to try to get in a quick bathroom break before the game started again. "What are your plans for the second half?"

"You're leaving that up to me?" Leo rolled closer. "The score is too tight. We should do whatever you think we should do."

"And I think we should do whatever *you* come up with . . . Captain."

Leo squinted at him. There wasn't much to captaining; it was just a title. Coach was the coach. Leo was who the players came to when they weren't getting along or needed advice on how to wrap their joints without losing circulation.

Coach cleared his throat. "Well? You're one of the most capable cadets in this skyscraper. And your mind is elsewhere, isn't it?"

"I don't know. Maybe." Leo felt too revved. Hot. Anxious. "You know why I can't focus. I'm working on a life thing right now."

"Then multitask. Scrape up something from the bottom of your imagination." Coach Vaughn started to walk off toward their newest teammate, who'd been in an accident last semester and was still getting used to the angled wheels on their sports chair.

Leo rolled farther away down the court, knowing that they didn't have to say anything for Coach Vaughn to hear their loud feelings. His aug fed emotions to him. It still felt so *off* that they weren't getting along—at least that's what Ace had called it.

Ordinarily, Leo would have played Vaughn's game. Come up with something and just said it. Did it. But it had been a *long* semester without Grayson.

Ace hopped over with a small cup and huge grin. He handed it to Leo. "The fourth-semester captain isn't playing! Did you see what she did to Phyl's wheel?"

Leo took the cup and sipped from it. They always got heartburn during the games, so water wasn't really their friend until it was all over. "Well, Phyl should tighten up his turns, and then he won't be such a wide-open target," they grumbled under their breath. It still felt odd to see Ace on the court, but he was overjoyed to play this minor role, his fame from his two flaps on SuperSoar further lifting his reputation on the skyscraper campus.

Most cadets would rather do anything else than play "water kid" on the sidelines, but luckily for Leo, Ace wasn't most cadets. He called it an upgrade from his role as mascot at his old middle school. He'd even been absolutely delighted by the team uniform, which had H_2O on the back, and had Leo take pictures to send to his moms.

Ugh, Leo wished this game were already over, and then they had to sit there for a miserable second with that feeling. They loved this sport. What was wrong with them? Did everything make them grouchy now? *Everything*?

"You look impatient," Ace said unhelpfully.

"Great, Ace. Thanks. Wait, you're not wearing your iNsight, are you?"

"What? No trial augs on the court. I follow the rules. Are you nervous because Grayson is watching?"

Leo spilled water all down their chin. "What?"

"Just, he never misses your games. Wherever he is, he could be streaming right now. This is the championship, Leo!" Ace turned his face up toward the high ceiling and waved.

Leo looked up, all around, but the media cameras were invisible at ToP. Only Otis knew where they were. They slumped in their chair. "Ace. He's not watching."

"But you don't know that."

Leo dared to wonder if Gray was watching their games. *This* game. But apparently Ace wasn't done messing with their nerves. "Well, Dr. Bix is *definitely* watching. He never misses a game. Gray told me that like ten times. He's a huge fan of this sport."

A tone sounded through the stadium, and the cadets who'd dashed away during the smidge of time between the halftime show and game were filing back in. Ace held up a hand for a high five, but Leo stared in the middle distance.

If the Bixes were watching, Leo needed to win.

And Leo knew how they needed to win.

While everyone shuffled into their seats and the music

blasted the stadium with *sit down* lights and sounds, they tucked the Sherlock aug in their ear, pretending to fix their sweatband.

The trial aug worked its magic faster and faster each time they used it. Their brain was getting so used to it. And their brain already didn't like *not* having it. In less than thirty seconds, Leo had it all sorted. Their teammates were tired. That meant the game was up to Leo, and to accomplish what they wanted—an audience with Dr. Bix to convince him to fast-track Sherlock surgery for them— they needed to win in a spectacular way. They popped out the trial aug and stuck it back into their pocket.

Leo wheeled out onto the court with the other players, beckoning their team to circle in a ball's toss away from where the other team had circled in.

"What are we doing?" Phyl asked, and that was the last straw.

"I'm going to score once to get us to that tie. Then we're going to hold the tie until sudden death at the very end. *No* scoring. We draw it out to the last second . . . and then I'll bring it in for the win."

Everyone stared at Leo. Two of their teammates' mouths gaped. Admittedly this was hardly the game plan that Coach Vaughn had been hoping they'd come up with, but it would be the most attention grabbing. If Dr. Bix was watching this game, Leo might have a chance to talk straight to him.

The second tone sounded to let the players know that it was time to take their positions. Their team cast nervous glances at one another, and Leo knew it was because they hadn't been given *any* real directions. Leo usually barked out one of Vaughn's strategies with those bizarre nicknames he gave them, like Sandwich King and Sandwich Socks. Sometimes they'd rehash the play to make sure the teammates were all on board with their positions and forward movements, but now the play was, what? Sandwich Leo?

Was this a brilliant idea or the worst?

Too many questions. This had become a haunting phrase in Leo's life. Too many questions, not enough answers. They started to daydream about what the Sherlock aug would show them about their life when they got to use it outside of that training room. Leo imagined it would be like a superhero movie where their vision sharpened with digital instructions deduced from new angles and intel. The best way forward would be clear, and they would always take it.

The way to Grayson would be clear too.

Save the green puppy.

Leo was nearly unready for the starting whistle from the ref. They snagged the ball, tucked it in between their knees, and shot down the court. It felt like the entire opposing team knew that Leo was the one to beat. They crowded all their wheels in Leo's way. A quick look behind their shoulder proved that half of their team was in position to press forward and score, but they'd hung to the sides.

The captain from the other team sped forward and slammed into Leo's wheels so hard that the plating over the spokes dented. It woke up Leo more than anything else, turning all their drive and frustration into fuel.

For solid minutes, they were on fire. They zipped and elbowed and twisted. They pushed forward a few inches at a time, grunting, breaking free.

And scored.

The ref blew the whistle, and the team regrouped. Leo felt like something in their brain was fizzing. They barked vague instructions, reminding their team to hold the tie til the very end so that the crowd could get their favorite part of the game after all. They repositioned, waited for the next whistle, and then shot into the fray.

The game pitched to a higher frequency as it built toward the tremendous excitement of sudden death overtime. It happened about every tenth game, and Leo knew that even if Dr. Bix hadn't been watching, he probably was now. They surprised themself by thinking about Stern and Rosa on that island, watching downloaded BEST-Ball games. What would Rosa see when she looked at Leo playing like this? Would she *know*? Maybe.

Leo decided that trusting Rosa was stupid. Only another Sherlock could trick them now. They shook the weird, powerful thoughts away. Good thing there was only Rosa, then Felix Danvers hidden somewhere, and the president.

Holy beans, would Leo become president some day?

It certainly seemed likely. They could be anything with Sherlock. Anything they wanted. Even Grayson Bix's paramour. *Whoa.* Where had *that* come from?

Leo flushed all over, sweating and shaking. They pushed their wheels into position for the blackout, ready. The stadium was full of green faces ready for the sudden dark.

When the tone sounded that loud, fierce countdown and the lights went out, Leo closed their eyes. They knew this place in their mind. They didn't need to see. They could hear where everyone was streaking in from the sides. They thought about Grayson, and that's how they made that final score:

Eyes shut tight, heart under pressure.

Leo coasted to the bench while the rest of the team celebrated as they filed into the locker room together. Thankfully Coach Vaughn went with them, and so Leo had like a minute to cool down before he grilled them on their moves. They knew he wasn't happy with their plays, win or not.

Ace bounded over, spilling water everywhere. "You were so awesome!"

No. I wasn't. I was a good player but a terrible captain.

"Find Emma for me, will you? Tell her I'll do a postgame interview for her gossip feed." Leo grabbed a towel from the folded pile and wiped down the sweat on their face and arms.

Ace didn't move, but his eyes got so big that Leo worried he was likely to lose his brows in his hairline permanently.

"Don't look at me like that. I know what I'm doing."

Ace scurried away, and Leo felt a sharp prick of disappointment in themself. They'd been so driven to find some way to get approved for Sherlock that they hadn't been paying close attention to Ace. After he'd become a SuperSoar star, he'd had to contend with a lot of celebrity-seeking friends. People were trying to use Ace, and he was too sweet to notice or stop them. Leo dropped a pin in that for later.

Ace was important to Leo, just not more important than Grayson.

Cue another sharp jab of unhelpful feelings.

Leo spiked up their sweaty, short hair and changed from their protective glasses to their square frames before their twin headed over. Their heartbeat pounded in their chest more tightly than it ever did on the court. They could do this. Emma was their sister. They talked to her *all the time*. Somehow this only made the anticipation worse.

Emma approached through the exiting crowds to where Leo sat at the edge of the court. To say that Emma looked suspicious would be an understatement on the grandest scale. She looked like she thought she was walking straight into a trap. "What are you doing?"

"We won. I'm going to give you an interview or whatever. For your show."

"Why?"

"Because you always ask me to, and today I feel like doing it."

"Why?"

Leo narrowed their eyes on their sister. The *why* game was one of Emma's favorites from when they were little. Leo didn't talk enough; Emma talked too much. Emma assumed this meant that Leo was hiding things. Being painfully introverted didn't count in their sister's book as a reasonable excuse for being so shy.

Leo missed Grayson. The feeling overwhelmed them out of nowhere in that moment and bright tears sparkled at the corner of their eyes, making the court feel like a place they'd never been before. They scrubbed at their face before Emma noticed, and the way she shifted to pull out her recording gear and sighed hard finalized that this interview was going to happen after all.

Leo could do this. They had to.

Emma's mini mic was cute and completely for looks. The handheld camera picked up sound nicely, but she liked to have something to maneuver between herself and her interviewees. Gray called it her *power stick*.

She held out the tiny ball of a camera strapped to her

wrist and pointed it at her face. That showstopper grin she'd spent years crafting turned on with a bright flick. "Welcome to the postgame celebration! We have a special treat tonight. I'm here with legendary third-semester captain Leo, who is special to me because, well, we have identical DNA!"

Emma turned the camera on her wrist so that it was taking in Leo, Emma, and the now empty court behind them.

Leo tried not to look straight into the little viewscreen that would prove they were very sweaty and scared looking. They tried to remember what Gray would do when cameras were turned on him:

Take a deep breath. Smile. Be confident.

Emma dropped her arm. "Okay, now you just look weird and unnatural."

Leo boiled for a second. Their sister was the only person on the planet that could do this to them—turn their body up to five hundred degrees in a flash. They were surprised, but not by the wave of strong feelings, but the words that came with them. *You make this impossible for me. Give me a chance. Why can't you let me be myself?*

"I'm . . . trying," they managed to get out.

"Just do your usual 'too cool for everything.' I'll take care of the rest." Emma put her camera-bearing wrist back in location and repeated her introduction. Leo tried for "too cool."

"All right, sib, you had one of the best games of your career tonight. How do you feel?"

Angry. Confused. Missing. So much missing.

"Spent," they said. Emma hooked an eyebrow and started to lower her camera arm again. "I didn't think I had that last score in me. I surprised myself."

Emma rolled her eyes and tapped pause on the recording. "*This* is your interview? You do realize you're supposed to actually say something of value. I might as well go stand outside the locker room and see if I can get some real emotion from the players who lost."

Emma turned to leave, and Leo snatched her elbow and yelled, "Could you give me like two minutes to try? This doesn't come easy to me!"

She dropped her camera smile for a hot minute. "Okay, fine. Take a minute."

Leo was overly aware of the way Emma watched them spin their wheels, turn their back, and think. They couldn't just say anything. They had to say something straight to Dr. Bix. Leo had to one-up the legendary man at his own game. What would the trial aug tell them to do?

When they turned back around they'd set their shoulders and chin. "Ask me the same question."

Leo had to give it to their twin. She reset her face and video with swift efficiency. "So, Leo, captain of the third-semester team, how do you feel after that compelling, down-to-the-wire win?"

"Relieved that I pulled it off. I planned the sudden death, but it all hinged on making that last throw. I could have lost the team the victory."

Emma seemed genuinely shocked. "You *planned* the sudden death?"

"I did. Coach Vaughn asked me to come up with the second-half calls, and I wanted to give the stadium something to cheer about. This is the last game of the season."

Emma still had one eyebrow out of sync with the rest of her face, and it made her look like a cartoon drawing. "So you kept your team from scoring until the last moment so you could pull off your tiebreaker move? That's risky . . . but bold."

Leo dared to hope that this was starting to go well. And then Emma kept going.

"Of course, this won't do much for the rumors that your teammates think you're a show-off loner who doesn't trust anyone enough to pass the ball." Leo didn't say anything; they didn't even blink. They weren't close with anyone on the team, and maybe that was weird because the rest of the team was *so* close. Leo had always had their boxmates; they didn't need anyone else.

Leo cleared their throat, talked a little lower on purpose. "The sudden death was all for Dr. Bix, who is a big fan of our games. Grayson Bix, his son, told me that those green-face celebrations are his favorite."

Could Gray really be watching?

Leo looked straight into the little camera on Emma's wrist. They smiled, looking more like their twin than they usually allowed. "Hey, Grayson." They waved at the camera before they could stop themself. "Miss you. Guess what? I picked my aug. I'm getting Sherlock."

Their heart pounded like they'd just finished a sweaty warm-up on the court. Dr. Bix would see that. He'd have to agree now that the news was out. Leo had played out a dozen scenarios in their head and in each one, Dr. Bix didn't back down from a dare.

Emma wrapped up the interview, popping the camera back into her shoulder bag. "Good finish. And *don't* we miss Grayson. My view counts are way down without his content."

Leo couldn't believe it was over. "I'm done?"

"You didn't do that bad. There's usable content there. I'll have to do some creative editing, but I think I have some old footage of you and Gray practicing on the court together. That stuff always gets the shares."

"You can't cut the stuff about me planning the sudden death for Dr. Bix. That's important."

Emma stopped trying to escape so fast. "Why?"

"He has to approve me for the aug. It's part of my plan for getting his attention."

"You're not smart enough for Sherlock, Leo." Her voice echoed in the empty stadium, heard only by the janitor bots sweeping up the trash and cleaning the bleachers.

Emma shook her head back and forth. "It's way too dangerous. Cadets have like literally lost their minds because of the trial aug alone! Hasn't anyone told you that?"

Leo opened their mouth, closed it. No one had told them that, but it did explain how wary the adults were about the aug. "How do you know cadets have lost their minds?"

"Because I *know* things. My job on this campus is literally a never-ending, globally fed, gossip stream. And I speak every known human language." Her smile was so smug. "You can't get Sherlock. I'll tell our parents you're going for the most dangerous aug. Don't make me."

"I'm going to do what I need to do."

The twins locked identical eyes for a hot minute, and then, like always, they went in opposite directions. As fast as they both could go.

15

INFIGHTING:
Enemies on the same team

It worked.

Not even three days after Emma aired her aftergame interview, Leo had a message from Dr. Bix's assistant asking to set up a "casual dining meetup." Leo had no idea what to wear to a dinner with the most powerful person in the world . . . who probably also stood directly between them and their best friend.

And who was also in control of their fate.

They opted for the velvet vest and pants they'd worn to the horrible Misey dance last semester. What a train wreck that had been. Emma saying they were crushing on Gray, and Gray getting all weird about it . . . Leo had nearly held hands with Siff at that dance, so yeah, mistakes were made.

But mostly their memory of that night boiled down to the fight with Emma. The twins hadn't spoken much since—which was quite a few months ago. When Emma had lived in a box twenty-four levels away, Leo hadn't felt weird about how little they talked to each other while at the program. Now Emma was twenty-four inches away on the other side of the wall, and they still barely spoke. And considering that Emma now knew every language on the planet—plus several animal languages—that was saying something.

Emma's PassPort trial aug hadn't helped her understand Leo *at all*, but then how could she understand a language that Leo was holding in?

Leo styled their messy, black hair in the mirror, leaning forward until their nose nearly touched the glass. They felt handsome in this getup. Confident. Ready. They added eyeliner and darkened their brows with a pencil.

"You will convince him to let you talk to Gray *or* get him to approve you for Sherlock. You can do this."

Ace knocked his "secret knock," which wasn't so much a secret as an obvious and particular way that Ace hammered on doors around the box. "Are you ready?"

"Maybe?" Leo spun on the spot to show off their outfit. "I'm glad Coach Vaughn will be there. I feel weird about a dinner with just Dr. Bix and me. Ace . . ."

"Yeah?" Ace was dangling from Leo's pull-up bar, straining in the neck to lift himself off his knees. Ever since he'd taken two flaps with SuperSoar, he was pushing himself to get stronger: to get to three flaps.

"Emma said something about cadets having problems with the Sherlock trial aug. Do you know anything about that?"

"Nope, but I could ask Otis."

"Otis won't know. Or won't be allowed to say."

"Don't underestimate Otis. There's something about that AI that's downright human, I swear." Ace dropped to his knees, staring at Leo sort of weirdly. "*Wait.*" He froze, eyes huge.

"What?" they asked. Ace didn't move, still solid with shock. "What?!"

"I bet Grayson's there with his dad. I bet they're going to surprise you. That's why he asked you to this dinner! Grayson's going to surprise you!"

Leo had a hard time not screaming some kind of nonsense sound at Ace. "That's . . . absurd. Why would you put something like that in my head? Don't say stuff like that, Ace. Geez. You know how much I'm dying to see him."

"Can I hope it?"

Leo wheeled out the room, unsure of what to think. They headed for the elevator.

Siff was in the common room, making a snack plate. Ever since he'd gotten his trial aug, he'd become a completely different person. Leo didn't know the particulars of his medical situation, only that he'd been in pain all his life, and all of a sudden, he wasn't anymore.

NerveHack was keeping him even-keeled.

Ace and Siff even played SAR together. The coffee table was all set with Ace's old, worn deck. "You two having a tournament?"

"He's teaching me. I'm getting good," Siff said matter-of-factly.

"You're okay. We're working toward *good*." Ace threw himself down on the couch. His attitude was such a complete reversal from his initial terror at living beside last semester's bully. At least it seemed like Ace had let go of the SAR card theft. Leo couldn't stop thinking that this was proof that the Resistance was kind of . . . extreme. Siff's aug was truly changing his life for the better; he was friends with people now.

How could augs be so evil that you need to live under water to escape them?

"Have a good game," Leo called back, but Siff and Ace were already debating who should deal. So much infighting there. Right before the door closed, Ace yelled goodbye and good luck so loud that Emma hollered for quiet from her room where she was listening to birdsong and attempting to mimic it.

All the way up to the level for Coach Vaughn's office, Leo couldn't stop thinking about Ace's terribly dreamy words: Grayson in his dad's office, ready to surprise them, not in any trouble after all. Proof that Bixonics was not evil, just too powerful like most successful companies.

The daydream was easy to believe. No wonder so many people didn't have the time or energy to think the worst about the biggest corporation on the planet. It was hard to admit that something that took up that much of your life wasn't right.

They itched to put in the trial bud, which they always kept in their pocket. On the one hand, having it in would mean understanding everything and making sure they could get what they needed. On the other hand, Vaughn had made it clear that using the trial aug outside of the training room was *not* okay. And for whatever reason, they still didn't feel bad about using it in the championship game. They held themself back with a lot of willpower.

Hold the course. Save the green puppy, they thought.

Leo had nearly arrived at the level for the teachers' offices where they were meeting Vaughn. They said *wait* so quietly that they were surprised when the elevator listened and paused between floors. It couldn't hurt to try Ace's patented technique: ask the AI. "What do you know about the Sherlock aug, Otis?"

Otis began to recite the vague information blocks from the Bixonics site.

"I already know all that," they said, frustrated. "What don't I know?"

Otis was silent for a moment. "The last seven cadets to be approved for the Sherlock trial aug did not graduate from the program."

"What?!"

The doors *dinged* and opened. Coach Vaughn was waiting in the hall. He was wearing regular clothes instead of his usual Bixonics-green tracksuit—which was weird. He grumbled a hello and entered. The doors closed again, and the elevator took them to the top of ToP.

So there had been more than three cadets who'd been approved for Sherlock . . . many more . . . but none of them ever went all the way with it. *And* Emma had reason to believe that something had gone wrong. She was overly dramatic at the best of times, but if Otis was right, those seven cadets hadn't just picked another aug—they'd washed out.

Why?

They pushed their doubts down with great force. After all, Leo knew this was a powerful aug—but they needed it for a powerful reason.

Ace's words about Gray waiting in his dad's office came back again, and all of a sudden, their heart was pounding and they felt red and unready to face this challenge. They glanced up at their coach and found him also red, because *of course*: he was picking up on Leo's nerves and excitement from even the idea of seeing Gray.

"It's hard to be around you these days, cadet." Coach Vaughn's voice cracked. He offered a small smile. "You're in pain. You've always been quiet, both in person and feelings, but this is different."

"So I'm not quiet anymore?" they asked.

Coach twisted a finger in his ear as if it might help tune the noise of all the feelings around him. Ace saw emotions via light auras; Leo wondered if Vaughn could *hear* them. "You're screaming on the inside, but then so is Dr. Bix, although the hologram distorts it. This is going to be a fun dinner for me."

An hour later, Leo was seated at the far end of a long, narrow table in a room they'd never been in before. Perhaps it was a conference room or dining place for administration. They sat on one side with Coach Vaughn across from them. At the farthest end, the hologram of Dr. Bix ate his dinner in jovial, static silence. They'd all exchanged a lot of pleasantries . . . but that was it.

Grayson was not there, of course.

Leo indulged in some mental images of sitting on Ace for putting that in their thoughts. They could barely eat, which felt automatically rude because Dr. Bix had found out their favorite meal—mac 'n' cheese with jalapeño—and had it brought up from the dining hall. He—or really his hologram—was dinning on something fancy. It was definitely seafood, most likely from one of those fish market aquariums that were so popular with rich people. Leo's family was well-off, but they couldn't afford a tank-grown lobster at the same price tag as a hoverpod.

Coach Vaughn surprised Leo by also being into the

spicy mac. Although every time he twisted a finger in his ear, they couldn't help wondering what he was picking up. Dr. Bix also seemed to notice.

"I had hoped Grayson could join us for this meal, but once he went off with his mom, he doesn't seem in a hurry to leave her." Dr. Bix smiled innocently. "Not even for us!"

"He missed her a lot while he was here. He didn't get a chance to see her once while he was in the program. She must have been busy."

Leo watched Dr. Bix flicker. They had expected the hologram, but the severe distance the scientist kept from Leo and Vaughn was new and different. His suit was impeccable as usual, but something was off. Why did he look so stiff? So quiet?

"I'm sure Gray's happy with his mom." Leo wasn't good at lying but planting words that might cause Dr. Bix to have an emotional reaction that Coach Vaughn could pick up on with his iNsight aug—that they were very good at.

Dr. Bix's response was to abandon his cutlery tools and pick up his lobster tail with both hands. He cracked it open with a snap.

Vaughn stared at Leo as if he knew exactly what they were doing by needling Dr. Bix about his son—and the coach did not approve. Which was fair. Leo shouldn't be trying to get info by bouncing things off one adult in order to see how it stuck to the other one. The Sherlock trial aug made their actions more impulsive than usual, less reserved, even when it wasn't in.

Dr. Bix tried to change the subject. "That was some victory a few nights ago! You had me dancing around my living room while I watched. That last score was . . ." He blew a chef's kiss.

"I did it for you."

"So I heard." His voice became quite a bit more serious. "And I imagine this has more to do with Sherlock, yes? I've looked over your test scores and agree that you might be an excellent candidate for the aug. But what I've decided is that you're too valuable. The aug is, in a word, risky."

"But I *know* I can be strong enough for Sherlock. And I know it's dangerous." It was a risk just to admit how much of a risk Sherlock is. Leo struggled with the words, but they'd gambled with their aug choice for far too long. It was time. "Dr. Bix, I know cadets have washed out after trying the trial aug. I know the president is one of the only people to be considered successful at integrating the aug into daily life."

"I would argue the *only* successful candidate." Dr. Bix wiped his mouth with his holographic napkin and set it next to his place setting. "And her life is hardly ordinary, isn't it? Tell me, great and powerful BESTBall champion Leo, what would you do with an aug as powerful as Sherlock? What would you deduce from the world around you? How would you solve . . . everything?"

I would help Grayson.

Leo didn't have a different answer ready. Their silence felt like a confirmation of their inability to handle it. Coach Vaughn was looking at them with his eyebrows set at their most serious position. He knew that Leo's attempt to get this aug was as one-sided and as stubborn as they were.

Dr. Bix continued through the awkward silence. "Leo. I reviewed your training profile, and I don't think this is the right gamble. What if we discussed all the different augs that I think you'd be an excellent fit for? Hercules, for example, would heighten your incredible skills on the court into the level of a superhero."

He should have aimed this dialogue at Ace, who still had his moments of believing that ToP was a program to create caped crusaders.

"What if I proved that I know the risks of Sherlock, and I'm still ready?" Leo found their voice slowly but surely. They rattled off a list of career applications and opportunities for human advancement with this aug. Technically Ace had put the list together, but it sounded impressive and well researched. Then they dropped their actual ace. "Plus, once I have Sherlock, Gray and I could do those Bixonics commercials together." They thought about the guards on the platform of Atlantis, with their BESTBall posters flashing ads. "People know me all over the world. We could show off together. That would be very good publicity, wouldn't it?"

The scientist leaned forward all the way over his plate. Leo had finally said something that Dr. Bix liked *a lot*. No doubt he remembered how much his son hated doing promotional material for his company . . . but Gray would do it happily if it meant being in the same room with Leo again, wouldn't he?

That's why it was such a good ace.

Coach Vaughn shifted in his seat. "The Sherlock aug isn't like Hercules. Once you have it, you'll be able to predict the immediate future, in a sense, and then you'll have the power to decide if it should happen or be changed. It would make you a nearly clairvoyant competitor on the court. An unfair advantage."

Dr. Bix laughed. "Clairvoyant! What a delightful exaggeration."

Leo looked to Vaughn; he was not exaggerating. They turned back to Dr. Bix. "What's the harm in letting me prove myself?"

And that's when Leo metaphorically shot themself in the arm.

Both of the adults suddenly had cloudy, dark expressions like they were remembering bad things that had happened to the last seven cadets who tried out Sherlock . . .

and then left the program un-augged.

"What about Mimic—" Dr. Bix started.

"I'm strong enough," Leo said. "I've proven that. Over and over. It's all I do at this place."

They took off the aug track bracelets they had been given at the end of their first semester. At the time, three options had been placed before Leo because they were more mature than the others; they'd had to get older faster than people who'd had everything handed to them like Emma.

They were capable, smart—and famous at this program and around the world.

And it was time to cash that all in.

"It's Sherlock, or I'm out."

For over a minute, Dr. Bix examined the remains of his lobster's shell, and Vaughn stirred his mac 'n' cheese.

"There would be stipulations," the famous scientist finally said. "Namely you would need to complete your training at Bixonics headquarters. It would mean leaving ToP and BESTBall behind."

"I'll do it." Leo hadn't even thought it through, but they'd come this far and if there was any chance of being reunited with Gray, it was at Bixonics HQ.

"Tomorrow, then."

"Tomorrow you'll decide?" Leo asked.

"Tomorrow you will have your surgery for Sherlock. It's time to move beyond the trial aug, *if* you're as serious as you claim to be. We best not waste any more time or energy trying to dissuade you."

Vaughn stood up suddenly. He looked from Leo to Dr. Bix and back again. Confusion and distrust flickered in his expression, but after that quick glance at Coach, Leo kept their eyes on Grayson's dad.

"I'm in."

JAYLA

LOOPS:
Rules of the code

[connectivity: Atlantis network, full access]

A great white shark circled the floor-to-ceiling windows of the undersea lab. Jayla kept one eye on the massive, open-mouthed beast while she worked. Why did she feel like it was spying on her? Bixonics might be powerful, but they didn't have control over sharks . . .

Yet.

Jayla grumpily slouched in her dad's chair. Rosa was asleep on the hovering cot at the center of the partitioned workspace. Her brow was all furrowed, even after taking one of Jayla's dad's powerful tranquilizers. It was easier for Rosa to be asleep while Jayla worked, so that her Sherlockian senses wouldn't overload with all the scientists and assistants popping in and out.

Jayla heard a commotion by the door, and at this point, she knew it was Grayson. The poor guy couldn't even walk around the Resistance headquarters without stirring up a lot of attention. He arrived at her cubicle with a bowl of chocolate gelato for Jayla.

"You're a lifesaver." She tore it out of his hands and had two bites in her mouth before anything else could happen.

Grayson stood next to Rosa, staring down at their growly sleep with an intense expression that Jayla didn't recognize.

"You okay?" she asked, mouth full.

"Yeah . . . it's just, it was so easy to be mad at my dad for all this. Feeling bad about what's happened to him and his company is . . . not easy."

"At least you're out of that locked floor now and your eyes aren't constantly making a movie for unknown viewers," she tried, although she probably shouldn't have because it did kind of imply that things were better now that his parents were *frozen alive*. Sheesh.

But Gray had always been good at skating on the surface of hard things. "Any luck with Sherlock?"

"The loops change too often. Like the software is protecting itself. I'm starting to think I'll need a Sherlock to fix a Sherlock, but Rosa gets overwhelmed too easily. What a bad idea this aug was." She paused. "Sorry. I know it was your dad's idea."

"My dad was . . . is . . . a big dreamer." Gray sat down a little glumly. "Mom used to say that sometimes big dreams are big nightmares. And you don't know until the end."

They had a moment when they both worried about the same thing. It happened often these days.

What if Leo found a way to get Sherlock like Rosa promised they would?

"We have time," Gray said. "They're only third semester anyway."

They had time. And boy, did they need it.

Jayla hoped the sugar from the gelato kicked in fast. She was so tired from lab work. Amir popped in from his own station across the lab, and the three former cadets started joking about the mashed potato gelato Jayla had tricked the ToP cafeteria bots into making when she was first learning how to write code for her aug.

Amir made a total *gross* face.

"Well, Ace loved it at least," Gray pointed out. "He invented some kind of chocolate gravy to put on top."

Jayla and Amir laughed together, and it made her glance at him from the side. Which was a big mistake because Grayson's VisionX eyes never missed anything. Her old boxmate grinned teasingly, and she threw her spoon at him.

The clatter and laughter brought Jayla's parents over.

"Any success, hon?" Jayla's mom asked while her dad checked Rosa's vitals.

Jayla shook her head miserably.

"They're going to wake up in a few minutes," her dad said. "Best to take her topside so she doesn't end up with a headache from all these people."

"Me? You want *me* to take Rosa to the surface?" Jayla was shocked. She hadn't been given permission to head up toward daylight in months.

"All three of you can go. You need some air, and we trust you."

Jayla marveled at that sentence for a long moment. Her parents trusted her now. They let her help, they appreciated her . . . it was amazing!

Her mom had a playful grin. "I also hear that Stern rowed his boat a few miles away from the satellite blocker so that he could download the BESTBall championship game."

Gray and Jayla exchanged excited glances.

BESTBall meant Leo.

At the surface, Jayla was shocked to find that it was night. Late at night. The ocean breeze was strong as she pushed the hovering medical cot with Rosa still asleep on it toward the small guard shack.

The surface of Atlantis was a strange place, all covered in inventive disguises. She'd done some research on the deepscraper as soon as she'd gotten the clearance to join the Atlantean network. When this place was in its heyday, it had been capped by a gleaming silver steeple. Now all that showiness was hidden beneath stretched camouflage canvases and strategic coconut husks. This had been a billionaire's baby, after his Mars colony failed. An under-water living community . . . that was sadly *not* tsunami proof. But Dr. Bix's money had fixed the broken seams and made it better.

The dark outline of Stern greeted them by the guard shack, where he was holding open the storm door with one finger. He had a big thermos of coffee waiting for Rosa, and she stirred at the smell alone. Within minutes, they were all hanging out on the bunks inside, watching the championship BESTBall game between the third semes-ters and the fourths.

Leo was on fire, and also, Jayla had to admit, not really playing like themself. They were more aggressive than usual, less aware of others. Leo had always been a fan of wheels-on-wheels collisions, but they'd hang around after the ref paused to reset things, making sure the other player and their chair were okay. This Leo slammed into people and wheeled away without looking back.

"They're distracted about something," Gray muttered from beside them. "They've got that distant look."

"There's Ace!" Stern cried. "The water kid!"

Ace seemed to hear them, waving at the camera while the two teams parted ways to head to the locker rooms during the halftime show. Leo darted a look straight toward one of the hovering camera drones. It felt, for a hot second, like Leo was looking directly at Jayla.

The second half of the game unrolled spectacularly,

building up to the sudden death. Stern surprised all of them by having the little green candies ready so that their faces could glow green in the dark along with those in the stadium during sudden death.

Amir was into it, adding this neon-blue lipstick that brought a lot of attention to his full mouth. Jayla grinned at him, and then turned quickly to Gray when her interest in Amir felt suddenly loud. Grayson seemed as distant as Leo. Amir nudged her elbow with his, and for whatever reason, it made Jayla's heart pound.

Rosa turned on the lights after the game. The aftershow started to play in the background, but for all that Jayla missed ToP and her box, Leo's gossipy twin was of no interest. Until she started interviewing Leo.

Gray didn't even have to say anything. Both of them stood right in front of the holographic projection that put a life-size version of Leo and Emma's interview in the room. Leo was sweaty from playing . . . but also clearly up to something. Their eyes looked shifty. Desperate?

Jayla got a bad feeling.

Emma's smile was so fake. "So, Leo, captain of the third-semester team, how do you feel after that compelling, down-to-the-wire win?"

"Relieved that I pulled it off. I planned the sudden death, but it all hinged on making that last throw. I could have lost the team the victory."

"*Planned* the sudden death?" Gray said, overlapping

with Emma's, "You *planned* the sudden death?"

Leo pushed their square glasses up their nose. "Coach Vaughn asked me to come up with the second-half calls, and I wanted to give the stadium something to cheer about. This is the last game of the season."

Jayla lost track of the interview for a second. Leo would never do that to their teammates. She almost missed the moment when Emma called Leo a show-off loner. Comments like that had always tossed Leo back into their silent, withdrawn ways.

Not this time.

Leo's voice dropped. "The sudden death was all for Dr. Bix, who is a big fan of our games. Grayson Bix, his son, told me that those green-face celebrations are his favorite." They looked straight into the camera and waved. "Hey, Grayson. Miss you. Guess what? I picked my aug. I'm getting Sherlock."

Jayla looked to where Gray had frozen into solid rock.

"You want to know the worst part of having Sherlock?" Rosa was kicking back on their bunk. "It's no fun to say *told you so.*"

"What do we do?" Gray asked. "Can we get them a message? Leo will stop going for it if I ask them to stop. They can't end up like Rosa." He glanced over his shoulder at the former cadet who was now imprisoned on this small island, dead to the outside world, still projecting a tracker that was only held at bay by Jayla's dad's satellite blocker.

"Oh, they won't end up like me." Rosa's voice was serious. "They won't make the same mistakes with Leo that they made with me."

"We still have time," Amir reminded the suddenly intense, stiff room. "Leo won't be going for their first surgery until fourth semester. They won't rush an aug choice like this."

Rosa laughed from the belly, and Jayla started to feel panicky. Gray was shifting around, nervous, upset, afraid.

"Gray, Amir and I know how to get out from underneath the signal dampener. We'll get a message to Leo ASAP. We can stop this before it happens. I promise."

"They need the batphone, Stern." Rosa was still half asleep thanks to Jayla's dad's medicine. Even so, their brain was already sorting out realities that Jayla could only sit and begin to imagine. "We're probably going to be too late."

Gray, Amir, and Jayla turned to Stern, alarmed.

Stern held out two patient hands. "Rosa is not always right, but we'd be fools not to listen. We have an only-for-emergencies line that directly connects to ToP."

Stern moved to the large, dusty control panel. He pushed some things around, while Jayla and Gray got as close as they could to watch. It took an excruciatingly long time for the connection to go through, and then we had to wait for someone to pick up. It was very, very early in the morning over at ToP.

When Ace's sleepy face appeared on a tiny, old-school

screen, Jayla pushed everyone out of the way to talk to him. "Ace! We saw Leo's interview after the BESTBall championship. They're going for Sherlock?"

Ace blinked, his hair standing straight up. Jayla realized with a jolt that he was inside the elevator. "What's happening? Otis woke me up and told me to come here, and I'm still asleep. Gray, is that you? GRAY! You're okay! Did you hear how I flew your hoverpod over the ocean?! Also, Leo helped me get some flaps in on SuperSoar!"

It was Gray's turn to push in. "Ace, we're going to catch up soon, but we need to talk to Leo. Can you go get them?"

"Nope." Ace yawned, light brown hair sticking up everywhere. "They're on the med level. They got approved for the Sherlock surgery yesterday, and everything's being rushed through. Everyone is so excited about Leo becoming the newest Sherlock! Although, wow, they've got a real attitude about it."

"Ace, it's *dangerous*." Jayla couldn't stop herself from glancing back at where Rosa rubbed her head. She was always tired, always overloaded with information, always worried about being discovered by Bixonics.

And that was the worst revelation of all: Bixonics was always going to control augged people. Jayla could disable their software, but they would adapt, evolve, make newer and more difficult trackers. Augs were definitely a huge leap in human evolution, but Bixonics was the worst kind of virus—the kind that leeched onto every good thing and took over every freedom.

"Ace? Are you there?"

The screen kept fuzzing and freezing. "Yeah, I tried to talk them out of it, but they made some deal with Gray's dad about being able to see Gray and work for Bixonics with him."

Gray's dad.

No, Leo hadn't made a deal with Gray's dad. He was frozen beneath the ocean. Leo had made a deal with Dr. Bix's hologram—with the unknown puppeteer!

Gray and Jayla locked eyes. It was go time.

The connection was breaking up. Jayla yelled, "We're coming, Ace. Stay safe. We're coming."

Ace's sleepy face and garbled voice disappeared as the connection broke up.

Jayla whirled around to face Rosa. "What's happening? Use that aug and *help us*!"

"Help? Sherlock doesn't help people. It predicts what they will do," Rosa growled. "It does not predict the actions of the corporation very well, and that is because of the special training."

"Training?" Amir asked.

"Cadets going for Sherlock have this brain-mapping training that keeps them from using the aug against the corporation. It literally goes offline when I try to tell you what Bixonics would do. I would never have escaped if Stern here hadn't knocked me out like a caveman and brought me to your mom and dad in his rowboat."

Stern was standing silently by Rosa. "They're my box-mate. I'd do anything for them, and when Dr. Bix tried to take them from ToP so they could go to the Bixonics HQ for more training, I couldn't let it happen. They'd already *trained* some of the things I love about Rosa out of them. She came back, though. Leo will too if you can get them away from all that brainwashing."

Rosa held out a hand to Stern, and he took it. Jayla's heart pounded.

"Give me the passcodes to the helo out there," Gray ordered, never sounding more like someone in line to take control of the largest corporation in the galaxy. "We're going to stop this now."

Jayla whirled on him. "We can't run off again with-out thinking this through. I *can't* do that to my parents. They've just started to trust me!"

"We can't wait!" Gray yelled.

"I'll get them and fill them in on the way up," Amir said. He disappeared toward the elevators that dropped down into the deepscraper.

"Suppose I'll make sure the helo is ready to fly." Stern followed Amir out.

Jayla couldn't help turning back to Rosa. She knew more than she was saying.

Why?

"What are you still not telling us about Sherlock?"

"I'm not telling you the things they made me forget."

Gray grabbed his head with both hands. "What does that even mean?"

"It means your Leo isn't in control of their brain anymore. Bixonics will take them to HQ, and once there . . . well, let's just say that the Resistance has been able to find a way to break into that compound. It's impenetrable . . . or maybe unreachable is a better word. They'll turn Leo into a tool for the company, just like the president. They won't even bring them back to this planet until they're sure they've got full control over Leo. Another powerful puppet for the puppeteer."

"Oh." Gray stood back, mouth hanging open, eyes wide. "Oh no. The station!"

"The *what*?" Jayla shot back.

Rosa sighed. "Yeah, little known fact. Bixonics HQ is the ultimate offshore asset. Located on the International Space Station."

17

RECURSION:
A problem broken into parts

Jayla's parents got suited up on the rooftop platform of Atlantis. Everyone was on full alert. It was midnight on the open ocean, and the breeze was cool, stirring up prickles on the back of Jayla's neck.

This was going to work. It had to.

Her mom and dad pulled on Bixonics jumpsuits over their clothes—the same ones they'd camouflaged themselves in when they'd rescued the boxmates a hundred years ago . . . which was also only a few months.

Gray was already getting strapped into the back of the vehicle, his expression unreadable. He was so worried about Leo. His feelings rattled through everyone.

Jayla felt sort of speechless when her mom held out a bundle of cloth. She took it, then unfurled a Bixonics uniform that was about her size. "You . . . think I should come?"

"We do." Her mom exchanged looks with her dad. "You've earned it."

Jayla didn't waste a second, pulling on the jumpsuit.

Amir pushed something small into her hand. "My lucky lipstick. In case."

"Thanks," Jayla said, and then she hugged him because she wanted to, and you know what? He seemed to want to as well. Jayla opened up a tab in her brain for that later on, when everything was less of an emergency.

Within a few minutes, the unbelievable was unfolding. The helo lifted off the ground, whisking her family into the sky and across the sea toward the jeweled beacon of the Tower of Power.

Jayla leaned against the window from where she'd waved goodbye to Amir, Rosa, and Stern.

After a while of watching the dark glitter of the ocean roll beneath them, she turned to her parents. "Why the uniforms?"

"Pretend to be the enemy." Her dad winked. "An oldie but a goodie."

"We've found that the uniforms inspire invisibility." Her mom pointed to the place on Jayla's shoulder that felt stiffer than the rest of the suit. "These jumpsuits have clearance badges sewn into them. A little bit like the hall passes we have in Atlantis to access the network and open doors. With a few strategic blackouts, we've been able to walk into the Tower of Power more times than we can count."

"These suits are worth their weight in tech gold," her dad added.

Jayla was impressed and intrigued, but another feeling elbowed its way in. "So you were in ToP a bunch of times while I was there, and you never came to see me." Well, now she'd done it. She didn't sound at all like a grown-up Resistance member, but a kid who'd been ignored by her parents.

"I checked in on you."

Jayla's head jumped up. "You did?"

"Of course we did." Her mom raised her chin, giving off that *ready for anything* expression that Jayla had been working to mimic for years. "I couldn't always be the person to go in, but we always made sure you were okay."

"One time during your first semester, I came to your box to fix your bathroom sink." Her dad grinned. "You didn't look twice at me. That was before you started rooming with him." He pointed at Gray. "That of course made it way harder. He was always under surveillance."

"I watched one of your swim practices. You were using the underwater breathing aug. What's it called again?" her mom asked.

"GillGraft. I nearly chose that one, but you know I've always loved tech. It's in my blood." Her dad bumped fists with her, and then Jayla peered out the window. The moment the helo was out from under the satellite blocker's protection, Jayla's aug reconnected with civilization.

[connectivity: full access to world wide web]

Jayla's network was going wild. Several apps that had been sound asleep during her time beneath the mighty blue Pacific had woken up. The sudden unfettered access to satellites and gigantic streams of global information poured through her, and she knew how Rosa must feel all the time. At least Jayla could turn it off if she wanted to.

Everything from the latest Hollywood nonsense to the newest fad diet was popping up in her mind, and she experimented with blocking them without her interface. Eyes closed, she focused, swiping away the ads and newsfeeds one at a time. The best XConnect users didn't even need an interface, and if Amir could do it, she would figure it out as soon as possible.

They weren't over water anymore, but land. A country flew by beneath them at unbelievable speeds.

"Fifteen minutes out!" the pilot called back.

"We go in the usual way," Jayla's mom was clearly in charge, something no one questioned. She broke down the plan for the boxmates as if mapping recursion, the plan and potential problems broken down into bite-size pieces. "*If* we get cornered or found out—"

"Then I'll do my thing," Gray shot in. "I might've been missing for a few months, but I'm still the junior VP of the Bixonics Corp. They have to listen to me."

Jayla's parents were a bit startled by how certain Gray was; Jayla wasn't. He'd been born to take charge of this corrupt company. Sure, he'd pushed against his destiny forever, not because he didn't want it but because he hadn't been given the choice before.

Now, it was his turn to make decisions. And he was going to step up.

As it turns out, the "usual way" for the Resistance to access ToP was to enter the basement tunnels from a block away, then travel all the way to the restricted sublevel fourteen of the skyscraper campus.

When Jayla's dad called the elevator with the button, she was a little surprised. "We're going up in Otis? Shouldn't we go some secret way?"

"The elevator is Resistance, didn't you know?" Her dad grinned.

Despite the situation, Grayson and Jayla chuckled. "Oh, Ace is going to be so smug about this when he finds out," he said.

But then the doors *dinged* and opened, and there was Ace asleep on the floor, surrounded by piles and piles of neatly sorted SAR cards.

He sat up and blearily looked at his old boxmates. They both weren't ready for the way he launched himself into their arms, immediately detailing his recent success with SuperSoar and worries about Leo, all in one breath.

Jayla's parents surprised her once again by hanging back in the elevator. "We're going to stay here." Her mom's voice was certain, no-nonsense. "We'll be right here, securing our quick getaway. Get Leo before the surgery starts."

Her dad put a hand on Jayla's shoulder. "If the procedure is already underway, they need to continue. It's too dangerous to stop halfway through. If they're already augged . . ."

He didn't have to finish that one. If Leo was already a Sherlock, they were all in big trouble. Leo had been to Atlantis. They knew *a lot* about the Resistance, and that would all be information the corporation could access, wouldn't it?

Jayla hugged her parents goodbye, then Gray, Ace, and Jayla headed up, up, up.

LEO

18

SQUARE OFF:
Let's do this

Leo was ready.

They were wheeled into surgery surrounded by med-bots and Bixonics physicians in full protective gear. For some reason, they'd always imagined that Coach Vaughn would be with them at this point, but he was missing.

Whatever had happened to move up the surgery, Leo didn't care. Soon they would be in a better position to help Grayson.

No, they'd be unstoppable.

They were ready to square off. They really were. That's what they'd told Ace when the surgery had gotten scheduled for the next day instead of the usual timeline and he'd sort of panicked. He didn't know all the things Leo now knew. And their training had been very clear that one of the hardest elements of Sherlock was the distance it could wedge between the augged person and the rest of humanity.

No one else could see the eventualities they could *nearly* understand with the trial aug. Even inside the seclusion of the training room, facts were facts, unavoidable and all part of the web of spinning truth. Leo now knew that they worked for that web. So did Grayson. And it was so much more important than boxmates or BESTBall games.

For one, the earth was swiftly becoming incompatible with human life. The signs were everywhere. From vast forest fires that ate entire states to atmospheric pollution that needed constant chemical treatments. People would need to colonize space a hundred years from now, and to do that they needed to be physically stronger. Bixonium would make that possible. It might seem like a kind of liquid radiation, making specific mutations and swift cell evolution possible, but it would save humanity with evolutionary leaps and bounds.

Leo had had a really hard day of training when they'd learned all the things that Bixonium can do on purpose. *And* by accident.

Shelve it, that's what the trial bud had advised, recommending they use the rigorous mental training they'd completed. *If the fact isn't serving you, shelve it.*

And save the green puppy.

The room emptied of doctors and surgery bots did their thing. Leo wished they didn't have to leave Ace to get this aug, but ever since he'd become proficient with

SuperSoar, Ace had friends aplenty. Not to mention, he'd been so worried by their change of opinion about Bixonics recently, but Leo's training had promised that that would happen. It was one of the named side effects.

And if Bixonics wasn't hiding it, it wasn't a bad thing. That tracked.

They were ready.

This was happening.

Their strict, sterile logic released their nerves and guilt about Ace. They didn't need to feel bad about anything because they were advancing their body and becoming an important part of the Bixonics family. This was going to help them save lives . . . so many more lives than just Grayson Bix's. If they protected Bixonics, Bixonics would save everyone. Even the people who didn't even know they needed to be saved.

Save Bixonics, save humanity.

The surgery began and darkness closed over them like a curtain shutting out the entire world, including themself.

PICK YOUR PERFECT AUG

BOD, BOOST, OR BRAIN

Aug Track: BOD
Where physical evolution is a *snap*

SuperSoar
Fly. Take off with style and glide on air currents for miles. Includes lighter bones and legit wings.

TurboLegs
Run as fast as the Hyperloop over great distances, no problem. Includes reinforced bones, joints, and ligaments.

VisionX
See colors you've never even heard of. Includes night vision and telescopic and microscopic zoom.

Hercules
Lift a hoverpod with one hand or do a thousand pull-ups without breaking a sweat. Includes reinforced bones, joints, and ligaments.

SonicBlast
Hear things no one else can or turn off annoying sounds—your choice. Includes new and improved echolocation.

HyperHops
Get the most powerful legs for jumping and swimming. Includes bonus joints and reinforced bones.

FelineFinesse
Never fall down again with a highly tuned sense of balance and increased spinal flexibility. Includes a tail, no joke.

Aug Track: BOOST
Where your natural strength gets *enhanced*

GillGraft

Breathe underwater for hours at a time. Includes new and improved internal decompression aid.

Scentrix

Super nose. Great taste. Increase your olfactory acuity. Includes new dampening mode to decrease sensitivity on demand.

UltraFlex

Be elastic, strong, and durable. Includes rubberized bones.

MegaMetabolism

Eat the whole cake or nothing at all. Survive in hazardous places with enhanced internal resilience. Includes an external gauge for switching between fasting and high-consumption modes.

SenseXL

Heighten all five senses at once. Become unstoppable. Includes new dampening mode to decrease sensitivity on demand.

DaVinci

Become your own muse with art as your first language. Includes superior dexterity and hand-eye coordination.

MetaMorph

Heal *fast*. Age slower and never get sick again. Includes improved cellular energy modifiers.

Aug Track: **BRAIN**
Where your mind becomes *unstoppable*

XConnect
Technology is your first language and fast friend. Includes an external interface for ease of transition and preliminary applications.

PassPort
Speak any language and master communication. Now includes several nonhuman languages such as dolphin, canine, and cricket.

NerveHack
Control your pain. Push your body to new levels without pesky nervous system restraints. Includes an external gauge for sensitivity transitions.

Mimic
Watch and learn; it's that easy. Includes increased mental storage to create your own database of abilities.

WeatherVein
Feel the tides, predict storms, and yes, catch lightning in a bottle. Includes rubberized bones for grounding during electrical atmospheric fluctuations.

Sherlock
Deduce, decode, and understand everything. Predict and detangle any mystery in a snap. Includes increased mental storage to create your own personalized database.

iNsight
Master the maze of human emotions. Achieve genius levels of emotional intelligence and empathetic influence. Now includes apathetic mode for on-demand sensitivity relief.

EXCITING
AND INSPIRING
STORIES

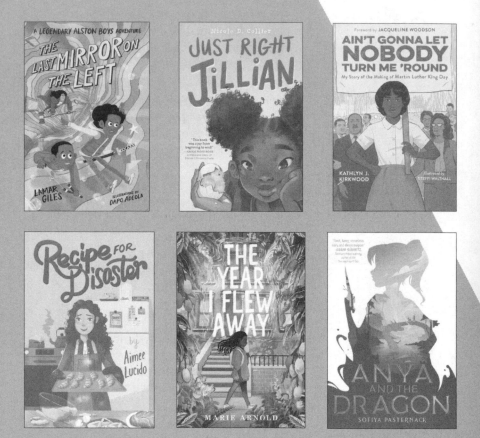

CHANGE THE WORLD, ONE WORD AT A TIME.